Francois Smith

The Camp Whore

Translated by Dominique Botha

Tafelberg

Tafelberg,
an imprint of NB Publishers, a division of Media24 Boeke (Pty) Ltd
40 Heerengracht, Cape Town, South Africa
PO Box 6525, Roggebaai, 8012, South Africa
www.tafelberg.com

Cover design by Michiel Botha
Cover photograph: iStock
Typography by Chérie Collins
Set in Granjon LT Standard

Printed by **novus print**, a Novus Holdings company

First edition 2017

ISBN: 978-0-624-08276-7
ISBN: 978-0-624-08277-4 (epub)
ISBN: 978-0-624-08278-1 (mobi)

To my parents,
Hendrik and Grietje Mor Smith

Chapter 1

He is lying with his back to her; his head is turned towards the drab, dead still curtains at the window. In the dimness she sees just a profile from behind: the ear a dark fold on the equally dark hunk of his head. If there was light, she thought, his ear would be transparent, rosy and fine-veined against the glare, the skin peeling perhaps along its wing-like curve. This is what she has been trained to do, to see light and life. That is her purpose here. But in the gloom everything is upended. Or perhaps exactly as it should be.

She pulls her gaze away to the shoulder protruding from the sheet and the arm lying limp on the blanket, the pyjama sleeve pushed up against the limb. The hand hangs over the hip, facing the front, out of sight, but the arm, the bit that shows, is thinner than she'd expected. What had she expected? Can she remember any of it?

She glances at Hurst standing next to her; he is staring intently and blankly at the patient on the bed. There is no escape, she has to look. At the soft creases of the cotton sleeve pilling at the elbow, the petal-like collar curving around the thin stem of the neck.

And again at the ear.

She does not feel surprised. Thus spake fate. The moment she set foot on these shores she sensed, within this vast unknown an ancient familiarity, that something – someone – somewhere, behind a façade, a door, a fence, was awaiting her. And now it was as if that realisation had led her eyes directly to the ear. That is what she noticed before anything else, the ear. That notch, like the incision a farmer makes on the ear of a sheep. And where you'd expect the soft fold of the lobe, the curve fell rudely to the neck.

That is her mark.

Her tongue sticks to her palate, loosens with a smacking sound. She turns to the door that has clicked shut behind them. She takes a deep breath, holds it a while before unevenly exhaling. How did I end up here? she wonders.

This is how it happened: She'd stood in front of the door, in front of that dark unyielding surface that is now behind them with its edge against the doorframe. She'd stood in front of that reflecting surface, the tiny varnish cracks like the retina of an eye, the smell of polished wood in her nostrils, her breath against that unforgiving surface, with eyes that she tried to tear away from the white label in the metal holder – the name that she cannot utter.

Major Hurst stood behind her, and she turned around, her face to one side so that he wouldn't see her shock, her fingertips pressed against the wood. Hurst had spoken, but what had he said? With one hand he gently pushed her aside, and with the other opened the door. Then she followed him into the dusk, the back of his smoothly ironed uniform between her and the man in the bed.

That is how it happened.

It is deathly quiet in the room. There is only silence. Until Hurst speaks. He'd stepped forward before he began to speak. He said the name of the man on the bed. The name she can't bring herself to say. And at the mere mention of that name, she feels herself seized, shaken, as if caught in a whirlwind – and hurled down at a litter of tents on the godforsaken Free State veld.

"Sister Nell?"

What? It is Hurst who has spoken. Here, right in front of her.

This is where she is, with Major Arthur Hurst in the Seale-Hayne Hospital in Devon. This is where she has to be, nowhere else; she must harness her will to remain present, here, in this moment. They are in the private rooms of one of the king's officers. No, not the king's – one of her own. Peering from behind Major Hurst, she can see most of the bed. The tips of two feet under a sheet. She blinks her eyes in an attempt to focus. The feet under the sheet give a nervous twitch.

Sixteen years ago she had lain like this in a twilight cave, waiting, lying and watching the shadow slowly shift across the mouth of the cave, lying and waiting and waiting and waiting for something inside her to calm down.

Chapter 2

I can see. My eyes must have been open long before I realised this. At first the light falling around me was so white that I thought it was not light, not light. I don't know what I thought it was, but whatever it was also poured from my mouth and everything, everything inside me and around me is filled with this bitter, burning nausea. I must not look; I don't want to know what it is, I don't want to feel like this, no, I don't. I don't. Everything must just go away. I must rather not think, because when I do my mind crushes me, my thoughts shoved up against the bone. It's the thinking that makes it crack open, makes it hurt so.

It smells of sheep. Dust and dung and stone and wool. I think I'm in some kind of cave. I'm lying in the shade, but at the open end the sun is so bright I cannot look. Speckled shafts of light, and farther on, dark people seem to be bending down and looking in, or perhaps it's rock rabbits among the wild olives. I don't know I cannot think my ears go deaf and all around me are paintings on the rock of people and animals and I hear the hooves of thousands of sheep on trampled earth they were the ones that stampeded over me all of them with their little sharp hooves grinding my whole body into the dirt flaying the skin off my cheeks off my ribs the hard horn in my eyes I cannot think I cannot think.

Now I know what I saw. My own thoughts. A bloody trail dribbling from my head, bubbling and gushing.

It hurts so much that I have tried to scream, but I can't, I just lie here. This is what I saw. I am lying like a slaughtered sheep with blue seeping veins bulging over the slimy white stomach, a blade grating, grating, a dried-out rusk falling to the dung floor and disintegrating where my toes should be, my mouth stuffed with sharp, hard crumbs. I can't say anything, because it smells of smoke and wool and sewage. Someone threw a cloth into that stinking ditch and I should rather look away, away, away because there are goats here red as soil and white like clouds they jump over each other in disarray people with sticks herd them black like mud are the people and the eland jump over me, jumping higher, higher, higher. If only I could shut my eyes so tightly that everything would vanish.

Chapter 3

The train clicketty-clacks sedately from Harwich through Devon's rich blend of green and brown, dissolving water-colours that trickle down the pane. But her mind still heaves with the swell of the grey sea and the ship's listless rocking, as if her thoughts lie sunken below the deep cold waters.

For most of the voyage she had stood on the upper deck of the mailboat to Harwich, one of just a handful of women among a multitude of men, mainly crew, some officials, even a few soldiers, all with a special concession to navigate the warring seas, which would otherwise be impossible. With the ferry services suspended, the mailboat was the only means of travel from the Netherlands to Britain.

The last time she'd been on board a ship was shortly before the end of the Boer War when she'd left Cape Town – ironically to get away from another war. The thought came to her there on the creaking deck of the mailboat with its wet voices and sea spray: *That war was mine. Not this one.* And as the boat pushed through calm seas that occasionally groaned into a swell, it occurred to her how different the North Sea was to the silver shimmer of the sea she remembered, whipped by the north-wester into thundering, frothing waves pounding against

the rocks at Three Anchor Bay. She briefly tried to recall something of *her* war, the one from sixteen years ago. By now she'd
been in the Netherlands almost as long as she had been in South
Africa. With some irritation, she pushed aside these thoughts.
It's over. My war is done.

What she does think about occasionally, almost reliving it
each time, is how young she was in 1902 when Cape Town
and Table Mountain had slipped from view behind her. Perhaps she should rather say she was young again, because before
that she was so terribly old, at death's door. How strange the
thought seems now, but that is how it was. On that day, on the
upper deck of the *Glenart Castle*, the cool metal of the railing
in her hands and the wind against her body, she was young.
That is the image she cherishes: removing her hat, pushing
stray curls from her forehead and for the first time, yes, it
must have been the first time, being aware of her blouse being
blown against her body, and how deliciously she *was* her body,
even now she can only find the Sotho word for it, *monate*,
delicious. She had grabbed the railing with both hands and
thrust her buttocks back, feeling the shock of her weight in
her arms, with the receding country and the sea around her
slap-slapping as she swung herself from side to side, and did
she sigh, did she sob? Actually no, what she remembers is this:
She was her body and that's as it should be; beneath her feet
she'd felt the cover plates shudder, the turbines pumping from
deep within the hold, with the faraway land from whence she
came growing faint.

And now she was on this boat, not unaware of what they
were sailing towards, not away from a war, no, on the contrary,

but her thoughts were full of the surf crashing on the Cape rocks, its almost frenzied energy, as handfuls of gulls were thrown into the moist air.

In the train through the British countryside she concentrates her mind to focus on recent events. She forces herself to retrace her steps, she believes in the value of being present in the moment, of not going through life blinkered.

She was on the mailboat, she had stood there in the embrace of an overcoat. The boat was nosing through a grey sea and grey sky, and that was portentous, because that boat, along with her, was bound for another, deeper darkness.

It had not fully dawned on her yet. In the Netherlands they live shielded from real violence. But on that boat … so ashen, as if everything had already been drained of life.

The deck was full of grey soldiers scurrying like ants, and if they'd come to a standstill, she now suspects, fear would have found a foothold. She had tried to imagine what they were up against, what the battlefield would look like, and what the men would be doing there. Looking at them, she tried to place one of the faces in a trench, a pale man with the sharply pointed nose and the bobbing head of a seagull. But she couldn't. Strangely enough, she could only visualise him lying with his back propped up against an anthill – yes, an anthill of all things! – with a long thin cigarette in his mouth and the smoke curling lazily upwards.

She tries to imagine the fear, the horror, but the closest she can get is the pale vacant face of her friend Jacques before he left again for the front. When she tries to picture the war, she thinks of Jacques. Jacques la Mer, her friend from

14

Dordrecht, a teacher set on becoming a soldier because his country, France, needed him. She'd once grabbed his hand as if to shake him awake, pushing his hand against her chest, but …

There is something upsetting and utterly unfathomable in that scene: Jacques's hand against her chest. His hand under hers. Her heart beating wildly. His face stiffening, his lips slightly apart as if he wanted to say something. His hand slipping slowly from hers and falling back into his lap.

She sees her eyes faintly mirrored in the train window. And behind the darkened sockets of her eyes, behind the dull reflection of her high forehead, her ash-blonde hair curling away and cascading down her cheek to her neck, she's aware of a sense of relief, a landscape that, unlike the Netherlands, if only because of the tilting horizon, its rise and fall, asks for attention. But she cannot quite look beyond her reflection, and it seems as if something skittish sporadically appears next to her mirrored image. Every now and then she glances to the side, but there is no one there.

This journey has me totally beside myself, she thinks. Why? I am here just to do my work. It's not as if I'm bound for the trenches.

She thinks again of Jacques; of the soldiers she's seen on the mailboat. She'd squeezed past one of them to get to the deck; it was actually a rather comical tussle as both of them tried to get through a door at the same time. For a moment they were pressed up against each other in the doorframe, its sharp edge covered in flaking paint and the black metal showing underneath. She recalls it as sharply as if it were happening now: her coat brushing against his uniform, and she looking past his face and seeing the peeling metal next to his ear, and they said nothing, trying only to extricate themselves as quickly as possible from a wholly unforeseen, totally uncalled for intimacy. Yet her body seems to shudder again from the shock of the soldier's body against hers, the uniform with its leather straps and clasps, the rough material and the hard metal, and below it the white, shuddering flesh, the smell of a bag filled with warm grain. After their bodies were freed from each other she'd taken a step back into the damp air, stood still, startled, not because of the unsolicited contact, quite the opposite, but why exactly, she could not say either.

That was also not the end of the bizarre dance – now the thought of a last waltz comes to her – it was just a prelude to something else, to something, yes, what should she call it, something far more sombre.

Up on deck, a group of people had huddled together against the railing, shouting and gesturing. She went and stood with them, next to all those men with their darting eyes, and looked at where they were gesturing into the fog, as if there were a fleck of colour visible somewhere. The mailboat sounded its horn, and then she saw it too: a ship looming from the mist, lifeless, lopsided in the water, unmistakably a wreck that might sink at any moment. The ship yawed in the water, rocking slowly in the swell, creaking, forlorn, metal plates peeling away from the bow, masts, smokestacks and cannons in rigor mortis. Everyone was transfixed. It was a ghost ship. She carefully turned her head, all the faces around her were petrified:

It was indeed a phantasm driven towards them by the wind.

She pushed through the bodies to the railing, watching hypnotised as the ship receded into the gloom. What on earth was it? What was that thing that appeared and then simply disappeared again? She looked around for someone to talk to, someone she might ask, but everyone suddenly seemed occupied with matters that could not be interrupted except on pain of death. She was faced with a wall of grey backs.

That is what this war is, she thought, a phantom in the mist, nothing more. It is not my war. Nothing here can take anything away from me. I am alive, and my role is to ensure that life triumphs. That is why I came here. But the image of the ghost ship stays with her, and oddly enough it does not upset her.

When the train entered Newton Abbot station, she felt that she could still hear the ship in the mist – a sound like the plonggg of cut barbed wire in recoil, she could hear it on the deck of that dying ship, the sound echoes and echoes and echoes. And she is reminded of the soldier she had brushed up against, his soft, yielding body, and the sharp metal that must have dug into his back, and she wondered, as the train lurched to a standstill, whether that dance with the soldier would be the closest she would get to the war.

She is one of two women disembarking here, and up ahead she sees a young man in uniform, probably one of the hospital orderlies, stopping the other woman, who shakes her head and looks away. The man laughs ruefully, sees her, raises an arm expectantly as he strides towards her.

She walks towards him holding her hand out in greeting.

But just before their hands meet, this being her first time on British soil, she becomes self-conscious about her accent. To him it should sound Dutch enough, she thinks, and her English is possibly better than that of most Dutchmen.

He listens to her, forlorn, as if he needs to make an effort to hear her above the din in the station, and then takes her largest suitcase. Jacobs is his name, Private Patrick Jacobs, with large front teeth, the cause, perhaps, of his decidedly nasal tone.

Jacobs walks ahead through the exit. In the street in front of the station, under the soft, low skies, he turns to her and sweeps his arm in an arc as if he were sowing oats, and there it stands, like a giant metal spider: a motorbike with a side-car.

She comes to an abrupt halt, sets her little suitcase down by her feet – or rather, drops it. It is inappropriate, she thinks, to react so spontaneously to the situation, but she nevertheless looks at the soldier with a smile. It is a Douglas. Yes, look, there is the name. Jacques had one of these, though without the sidecar. Such a pest, following her abroad like this. She steps forward and draws a finger across the cool round lid of the sleek petrol tank, takes hold of a cable on the handle-bars, slides her thumb and finger across to … ah, the clutch! Jacques was oh so proud of his clutch, one of the very first. She gives the rubber bulb a light squeeze, and as it honks she glances up at the British private watching her with a be-mused smile.

What she knows about motorbikes she'd learnt from Jacques. Jacques la Mer, a Frenchman in Holland. The French-man-with-the-motorbike. That Saturday morning of her first weekend in Dordrecht she'd heard a noise in the street, quickly run to the window and seen a man sitting legs astride the monster. He'd looked up at her and made the engine roar. She felt butterflies against her belly.

The private picked up the bag behind her. "It's about three and a half miles to the hospital," he said, looking up at her with a wry smile as he bent down. "Let's enjoy life while we can, don't you think?"

Then he laughed loudly, rather derisively, and fastened her luggage to the tailboard. He shoved a pair of goggles into her hand and held his elbow out to steady her as she climbed in.

Enjoy life … What does he mean, exactly? But the orderly is already battling to kick-start the engine — at least, that is what she presumes. She's seen it before, the kicking, but with Jacques's motorbike you had to push-start and then quickly jump on while running. Prrr, prrr, prrr, he kicks, and she continues with what she has been doing ever since Harwich: trying to concentrate on what is going on around her, trying to get a grip on the landscape, the buildings, trying to comprehend this part of the world.

Is there really a war on the go somewhere? And why is it not evident? There is nevertheless a strange, vague sort of disquiet in her, not exactly relating to this country and its war, but rather to her inability to concentrate fully on anything outside of herself. She is plagued by a persistent feeling that there is something else, just out of view, that actually merits her attention.

Jacobs's unrelenting kicking does not make it any easier, and before she knows it her gaze is fixed on the blush rising from his jaw across his smooth cheeks – without a trace of beard – and the uniform jacket bouncing up and down above his seat. Oh, dear Lord, even in that she sees Jacques. But the fact is, even when she was driving the bike, in Dordrecht, he first had to warm the engine before they could push-start it, pumping at a lever on the engine. And now, in this strange town in this strange country and with a soldier who is a total stranger under orders to accompany her, this is what rises to the fore: how she sat on the back of Jacques la Mer's motor-bike put-put-putting along little paths through Biesbosch's reed and grass meadows. Later, she drove herself, but he first had to show her: here are the gears, one, two, three; there you slowly release the petrol; get your fingers properly around the brake.

Back and forth, they charged along the paths of Biesbosch, with her unsteady on the tailboard – through the sea breeze, through shafts of sunlight and shadow, gasping as they descended into bogs filled with cool air to suddenly emerge into languid clarity, her hands under his coat, his jerking ribs below her fingertips, below the pumping lungs, the headlong rush of blood. Reed-cutters pulling themselves upright and gesturing with their sickles; she, laughing loudly, deliberately, scornfully into the back of Jacques's head, and feeling him flinch. Yes, that she remembers now, how often he shrank from her touch.

Why would she remember that now ...? Once, after they'd driven back to the apartment, Jacques remained seated, his hands clamped onto the handlebars. "What's wrong?" she asked. "Are you coming in?"

He did not look up, it was as if he were talking to the motorbike. "I don't think we should do it," he said.

"Do what? What are you talking about?"

He climbed off and pushed past her. "You know only too well," he muttered.

She stared at his back. His long, duck-like strides, his sunken shoulders. Poor thing, she thought, and recoiled, as if it were he who'd turned and hurled the words at her. Poor, poor thing! But he had simply walked up the stairs and let the front door slam shut behind him.

Jacobs swings his leg over the sputtering motorbike's saddle, glances at her over his shoulder before slipping into gear and roaring down the street. The momentum pushes her against the seat; alarmed, she glances first to her left and then to her right and grabs hold of the rim of the sidecar. She thought she had already figured it out, that thing with Jacques, but it kept churning in her thoughts as houses, people and trees flashed past, a strange, strange confrontation. After all, there had been nothing between them. He was an occasional companion of sorts. Yes, that's the word, companion. Perhaps the problem was that the occasions had been determined by her, and by her alone. Anyhow, that's the conclusion she had come to: that he had found her too presumptuous, too controlling. But now she wonders. Once again, she sees the reed-cutters slowly standing up, their sickles swing, she hears the blades slicing through the grass, she feels his trembling skin under her fingertips. He must have felt it too. But what, exactly?

Out of the corner of her eye she sees a great structure flashing past and she turns her head: In the middle of the street is a clock tower, squat, massive, seemingly the remains of a collapsed church, the ruins half-covered in ivy, but with the clock intact. Now her attention is again fully focused on the surrounds; she is aware of the bumpy, noisy motorbike with the soldier holding on to the handlebars. A commonplace sight, it seems, as a man pushing a bike does not lift his head, and people walk along the street lost in thought. She presses her cloche tighter against her head, and with the other hand holds onto the rim of the sidecar.

Jacobs points out the landmarks along the way, the sights, things she should know if she'll be living and working in this community for a while.

Once or twice he stops at a crossing, pushes up his goggles and delivers a schoolboy explanation: the house where some cricketer was born, the hospital staff's favourite bar. Some of the nurses come here, he says with the croaking laugh she'd heard earlier. She laughs with him, totally receptive to his excitement, leaning forward and speaking loudly above the roar of the engine: "I probably won't be able to come without a companion."

"I am sure that can be arranged," he says and winks.

She looks away. Suddenly annoyed. She has allowed him too much; she encouraged him. She hears him speaking, but intentionally diverts her thoughts away from him, away from all boy soldiers on motorbikes. She knows the excitement, the inherent daring in the union of man and machine. Carefully now, carefully … she feels a prickliness crawling up her sides and glances at Jacobs. He has been watching her all along, she realises, but he looks away quickly to something he imagines has attracted her attention. He searches around, and then, nodding his head, he says, "No, I don't know, they're just ordinary houses."

She laughs, relieved, dismissing her question with a wave of the hand, stretching an arm towards him and flicking her fingertips: Drive, just drive.

On the outskirts of the town he stops once more, lifts the goggles over the shield of his cap, rather laboriously takes the motorbike out of gear, rests an elbow on the handlebars and indicates with a long forefinger: "Do you see that house?" he asks, and points to a row of pitched roofs, terraced houses jutting from behind a newly built circular wall. "The one on the far left is where one of our greatest generals was born, Leslie Rundle." He allows the name to sink in. "Fought mostly in Africa. Against the Zulus, the Boers." He nods approvingly at the white façade with the single sash window visible above the stone wall.

Her gaze, which moments before was still gliding, flicking freely along walls and roofs from horizon to street level, is suddenly arrested. She turns to look, feels her discomfort become something else, not irritation exactly, although Jacobs's undisguised admiration makes her think for a moment that she is reacting childishly. Something else however stirs in her consciousness; for some or other reason she does not succeed in giving herself over to this landscape with full attention.

For a good mile or so on the bumpy road out of town she tries to overcome this dead-end, this darkening of her gaze. Later she tried to recall the journey, trying to remember what she had seen. Leaves gathering against low stone walls;

a woman leaning out of a window, arms spread wide as if asking for money; trees spreading their branches across the road in an almost exact re-enactment of her gesture. Images following one upon the other.

Jacobs starts to slow down and nods at the building in front of them, but she hardly notices the hospital lying up ahead. She does notice the turreted gateway, but her thoughts keep turning around that white terraced house, over and over again, like a gear that keeps slipping. It's unusual; she is not one for digging into the past. Impulsive, yes, often even impetuous, but she does not get bogged down in things.

She can hardly wait for Jacobs to complete his wide turn as they come to a standstill right at the entrance. She climbs out of the sidecar and starts speaking immediately. He is still pondering over the last snort of the engine, or busy with one of those studied intimacies that exist between men and their machines, when she almost shouts at him: "Why did you show me that?" She sees him look up, startled, immediately loses steam, but takes a deep breath and tries again: "Why did you show me that house?"

He obviously doesn't know what she's talking about. "That house?"

"Yes, that house. That belongs to the general. Why?"

He removes his goggles slowly, and that lazy, carefree gesture is all it takes to bring her to her senses. Only then, and at a distance, can she hear herself and see herself standing there in a new world – woman, man and machine, and behind them the large hospital.

"Never mind," she says and takes her suitcase from him.

"Never mind." And she turns around and walks into the hospital for the very first time. How could I? she thinks, and she knows that Jacobs is staring at her. I am completely daft. She lifts her chin and strides away from the clear afternoon light into the hospital's shadowy arches.

Chapter 4

It's easiest to lie on my side. My head, at least, is on a folded sack of sorts, and below me is a dark-coloured blanket that has probably been spread over flattened grass. My body is not shaking now, not now, but I know that the spasms will keep coming. It's too painful to move my head. Also, my eyes are still full of what feels like rusk crumbs.

My thoughts come to me more clearly now, but mostly just eddy away. Like the mud at the bottom of a rock pool becoming a brownish cloud as you put your hand into the water, unable to grab hold of anything.

If only I could get hold of something to quench this terrible thirst, but how can I drink when my mouth is full of sand? What could I drink?

It hurts. It stinks. There is light, yes, there is light. There are also noises. A red-winged starling. Cher-leeeoo-cher-leee-oo is its call. I remember that.

Rock. Above me and around me. I am in a cave, I know that now. On the rockface eland are leaping over me, and between them are little black men with knobkerries in their hands. I also know what that is.

On Bosrand there was a cave with Bushman paintings.

Yes, Bosrand. Now things are coming back to me. Pa had shown us. Pa. Ma. Neels. Me.

There was also a face in front of me. I remember now. And the shock. He sat on his haunches next to me, and I saw the grains of sand on his pants and on his hand. Then I saw that the hand was black. I closed my eyes. Shut them. Later on, I again tried to work out where I was but all I could see were these mud clouds and the only thing that existed was this terrible fear.

It's also him talking now, that face. It's like rocks tumbling down a mountain from up high. It is a sound that I know. I understand what he is saying. *Kgotso, Mofumahatsana*, he says. That is how they greet one. The good ones, that is their greeting. But he just wants me to believe that he is one of the good ones, what he really wants is a white woman to do with as he pleases.

I can see him clearly now. He sits with his knees pulled up and holds a knobkerrie between his legs. His head is turned away, but I know he is watching from the corner of his eye. *Metsi*. That is what I need to say. Water. I want water. He must give me water, that is all I want, and then I can die. He must just kill me quickly so that I cannot see or feel what he is doing.

He puts the knobkerrie down and stands up. I'm scared half to death. But all he does is dip his hand into a calabash next to me – I've only just noticed it – and bring his hand to my mouth. Cupped.

I stick out my tongue and can at least taste the water. He lets it drip. I try to swallow, but my tongue won't move. Luckily, more comes, and then more. The water is bitter, tasting of leaves, something like aloe or sage. My whole face is wet, and so are my chin and throat.

There is something wrapped around my head, I can feel that now. Why am I lying here under a blanket? Am I naked? What has this herdsman done to me? What is he going to do to me?

O mang? That is what I should say. Who are you? But the words refuse to come out. I can't speak. Like Ma, when she tried to pray but couldn't find the words and stretched her hands out towards me. Lord, watch over us, and let your light shine upon us.

My lips crack when I try to open my mouth. Only prayer will prevent darkness from descending on the land. I am Alpha and Omega, the beginning and the end, sayeth the Lord. There is a priest sticking his hands up in the air, straight as an arrow up at the clouds and he looks down at me, and I look away from his terrible face, away from his eyes glaring at me like a glowing furnace, seeing only evil and wretchedness. Where is that herdsman who is always sitting here, next to me, where is he?

His name is Tiisetso. He doesn't call me *nooi*. But then he looks away and says *ke sôno*. It's a great pity, he says. He says I must sleep again so that I can become strong again. He says I was hurt badly at Balla Bosiu. With his knobkerrie, he pounds the ground between his feet.

Balla Bosiu. The camp. The place where they weep at night, that is what they call it. That I do remember. The camp. That is where I have come from. I know that now. But if I close

28

my eyes and think, then all that comes to mind is the feel of a sheep's hoof in my hand, how hard the bone is under the skin, and the prickly wool, and the kick that jerks my arm right up to my shoulder. Then I see someone pull back the head and swiftly draw a blade across the throat and cut, cut, cut as the blood bubbles and the windpipe bursts, and I cannot look away even though I want to and the man who is slaughtering looks at me, his nose is thin and skew and his lips are dry and the same colour as his skin, not red, and he says something to me, but I cannot hear what he is saying.

Instead, I keep my eyes open.

But how did I get here? This man must tell me. What is he going to do with me? If only I could ask. What is he going to do with me?

Chapter 5

Afterwards, long afterwards, the thought occurred to her that her whole life and everything that had happened to her had culminated in that exact moment, in that instant when she reached for the handle, lifting her hand to that doorknob from under the dead weight of time – everything had spiralled towards that door and what lay behind it.

But she needed to calm down before she could see clearly: her presence before that door and how she'd come to be there. Strangely, it had happened long after she'd lost her faith in a natural order of things. By then she was already a full partner at Reymaker Psychiatrie, and the gap between what she theoretically believed in and her instincts had eventually narrowed to the point where she could practise her profession freely with an open mind. Though with a certain Dutch insouciance – no, instead she did so in an almost constant state of anger, impatient with frivolities. She had been completely assimilated. How else, she looks so Dutch: her face open and glowing, flaxen hair that she often rolls into a bun so that the old scars on her forehead are visible, the days when she'd so diligently hidden them long gone. Furthermore, she is tall and not at all fragile, her mouth is wide and full – rather greedy, this mouth of mine, she sometimes thinks when she allows herself to be self-critical. But she guards against that; too much self-criticism does no one any good, neither you nor those around you. And when she looks at her eyes, today still, she knows to be careful: you are not as strong as you think you are. She can be wilful. Probably the reason why she allowed her Dutch to retain an Afrikaans hue. Pure wilfulness. But then obstinacy is a known quality of the Dutch. So, where does that leave one?

One thing's for sure, she's far more at home with business-like communication. That's if she compares it to the idle chatter she'd grown up with, the conversations and things. Her interaction with patients is direct and to the point. She would, for example, firmly silence a whining patient and say: Come, let's separate the wheat from the chaff. The woman she's thinking of was so consumed by neurosis that her melancholy, pessimism and obsession with death had led to the murder of her husband, almost as if she'd challenged death. To this woman she had said: You don't dare think like that. The world is utterly indifferent to you, pays no attention whatsoever to what you think or do, or to what happens to you, or for that matter to what happened to your husband.

Strange that she should be thinking about this now. It's early evening and the office has been quiet for a while already. In fact, her whole life is quieter now. The frenetic bustle is over. It's not so much a case of waning strength, but simply the desire for silence. To be honest, she can now face silence. Only now. And so she spends more and more time in her office after work.

31

Quietly at her desk, before its smooth empty surface. She tolerates nothing on her desk, not even a book or a reading lamp, and when necessary takes a notebook out of a drawer. The walls, however, are an untidy tapestry of books, ornaments, artworks: a ceremonial mask from the Congo, a framed print of a clay pot and a woven mat brought to her from South Africa. This is her world; she finds the contradictions comforting. That is how she wants it. And it was here that she'd first seen herself in front of that door, realising that the world, her world, against all logic and without her realising it, had assumed the shape, the contours of that scene. As if the world in some macabre way was meddling in her affairs.

For a long time it was impossible, but now she can follow her train of thought, these days she can face it. The ride with Jacobs in his sidecar. That room in that hospital. And one of these days, she knows she will be able to face going back to where it all began.

The hospital is a fortress-like building, with red brick and ornamental plasterwork; the entrance is an archway below a watchtower with parapets. She emerges from the shadowy doorway into the blinding light of the morning sun reflecting off the ash-white gravel and the windows encircling the courtyard. She walks with her chin pulled in, giving the impression that she literally has to rein herself in.

It is not a graceful gait, but the rhythmic movement of the shoulders, from side to side, makes it seem as if she has dancing in mind, or even a soldier's march. She walks lost in thought, her serene expression contradicting the pent-up energy of her stride.

Yesterday Jacobs showed her where to report. Hurst, the hospital chief, was not available then, and Jacobs's careful knocking was met with silence. The hallways were nevertheless full of hospital activities, women scurrying around in nurses' uniforms, a few deigning to throw her a sideways glance. From a corridor window she'd looked down on an overgrown garden. She'd seen two men in uniform walking in the shrubbery.

This time there is an answer when she knocks. He is sitting at a writing table watching her enter, and appears to be made of wax. For a moment she is convinced it is a wax statue, even though she should be used to the fact that European men look so different to the ones she'd grown up with. How freshly scrubbed they looked. Dr Arthur Hurst, however, looks almost transparent, his hair greased back and shiny, his top lip a taut line above the fleshy, mobile lower lip. The bottom lip and the eyes, she thinks, are the only parts of his face that have not been painted onto the blank visage with light brushstrokes. The eye sockets and the bottom lip have been roughly fashioned from potter's clay, with a finger and thumb, and you'd need to be much, much closer to see what's been put into those hollows.

As he rises from his desk, his voice comes from deep inside the curve of his body. "Seeing is believing," he says in a tone that reminds her of the guilelessness of some of Jacobs's hand gestures, and she feels an apprehension stirring within. "You are indeed a woman." He walks around to her, his hand

33

half-raised for a greeting. "I almost fell on my back when Rivers said he was sending …" His mouth falls silent, narrowing to little more than a skew sheepish pleat on his face.

"Would you have preferred a man?" she says coolly, after shaking his hand. She realises that it was his undisguised embarrassment that gave her the courage. Therein lies his charm.

"Lord, no, please don't get me wrong …" He gestures towards a high-backed office chair. "Please sit down."

He is in uniform. Not the khaki she'd become familiar with in South Africa, but an olive-green duffel fabric. The Sam Browne belt with its lanyard across the chest she knows well, and the puttees too. As he walks back to his chair, she also recognises the measured, deliberate steps that the puttees give to the wearer.

She is in her Dutch nurse's uniform, and when she drops her chin she feels the cool bakelite of the yellow cross on her high collar.

She smoothes the white pinafore over her thighs, and at this moment, in this office and under the gaze of this man, she recalls of the only photograph of herself that she likes: her face angular rather than flat, her wide mouth with its pinched corners curling in barely perceptible scorn. Her face is turned away from the camera so that a shadow falls across the left side, but why she likes that photo most … no, "scorn" is not the right word, she's not that way inclined, but there is nevertheless a certain defiance that she radiates. Or is it simply that she'd managed to completely ignore the attention of the camera?

34

When Hurst speaks again, she's half-startled; for a moment she had been entirely lost in her thoughts. "After all, you are not the only woman here," he says, though without any sharpness. "The place was also, and not so long ago, the headquarters of the Women's Land Army – we've been here for, oh, barely a year."

He stops speaking and watches her expectantly. She feels herself blushing involuntarily, and looks down at her hands in exasperation, hoping he has not noticed. But when she looks up at him again, he has leant forward in his chair, his elbows resting on the table.

Her reaction was evidently acceptable, or at least not suspect, because he now speaks with a noticeable uplift in his tone of voice: "Our warriors of the ploughshare. You must have heard of them, even perhaps come across them? How long have you been here? Oh, it doesn't matter, the fact is the place is actually an agricultural college ... or rather was, before headquarters decided it was more important to get shellshocked soldiers back to the front than to train women to take their place in the farmlands of the kingdom."

Ah, she knows what he is talking about! She wonders for a moment whether he was being sarcastic, but his face betrays nothing. Now she knows why she blushed. Yes, she knows: when she was on her way to the hospital in the sidecar this morning they suddenly filled the road, these women. She'd grabbed hold of the sidecar, and felt Jacobs brake sharply. It took her a while to understand what she was seeing: the short overcoats, the pushed-up breeches, long grey socks, blue jerseys tucked into trousers, a couple of rubber boots, and here and there a hoe casually resting on the shoulder. But the hips and thighs and hair and breasts – they were indisputably women!

The group of labouring women, farming women, had given way to the motorbike in playful haste, with exuberance, even. Jacobs had accelerated and sped past and she tried to look back at the jubilant group, but Jacobs was trying to shout something at her above the roar of the engine, and she'd pulled her head back and leant across to him. He almost had to bring the bike to a halt before she could hear what he was saying and understand what his cackling laugh meant, his mouth agape and his tongue … yes, now that she thinks of it, it was quite obscene, the way he'd flapped his tongue between his teeth. She'd quickly looked away from him, stared intently at the road ahead, clinging to the flanks of the sidecar as they careened and bumped their way towards the hospital. Confused, she tried to make sense of Jacobs's reaction to what they'd just seen. And above everything there was this strange anxiety inside her. There was something inappropriate about those silly women in men's clothes, but – and this is what made her blush again – something deliciously exciting too.

She realises that Hurst is staring at her with a furrowed brow, and she looks down at her hands again. She is truly embarrassed by her reaction now. And why exactly, she does not know, because it has nothing to do with her.

It must be the strangeness of it all. The country is strange; she is a stranger. Yes, suddenly she even finds herself a bit odd. But then she hears Hurst speak and looks up halfway through his sentence and, noticing his questioning gaze, she tries to smile.

"I realise it is quite controversial, and to you, being Dutch, it must seem all the more strange."

Dutch? Did Reymaker not let them know that she was a South African? Or had been. But now she is not at all sure what Reymaker might think others need to know about her. What would he have let them know? He must surely have spoken to his friend Rivers about her, because that's how she ended up here – he'd facilitated the introduction. And what had Reymaker told Rivers? Do you have room here for a woman, and – don't laugh – one with an interest in shellshock?

Oh well, it was not shellshock per se that had lured her here, even though Reymaker thought so. Or, rather, he thought she had some kind of morbid interest in the war. That's what he threw at her the first time she told him about her "war plan". When she asked him whether there might not perhaps be a position for her in one of the British military hospitals, his answer was: But it is not our war.

Indeed. It is not "our" war. Not even the fact that South Africans were being trampled into French mud made it her or Reymaker's war. Their war, hers and Reymaker's, was there in their clinic in Dordrecht. Their daily battle was to give a few people a grip on reality, perhaps even a grip on meaning.

On happiness? But that is not what Reymaker meant. He was simply alluding to the fact that the Netherlands was neutral, and not part of the war.

Or is that really what he meant? Reymaker had collapsed

into the chair behind his desk, behind that bronze statue of a seated cat. His beloved cat. He'd peered past the cat at her; his eyes steady and coal-black above his sparse beard. She had remained standing with her hands on the back of a chair. Through the window she could see a rippled canal, on the skyline the squat spire of the Grote Kerk and fleecy clouds that seemed strange to her, even after fifteen years in the country. But to Reymaker and his peculiar habits, she had long grown accustomed.

She tried again to explain why she was so interested in the work of Rivers. It was not as if Dr W.H.R. Rivers's approach had any specific connection to Africa, even less so to South Africa, but something that appealed to her from the outset was that his work was based on his research on traditional medicines of primitive tribes. She couldn't believe it. Superstition! Magic! Witches! Those were all swearwords in the world where she lived and worked – and yes, she did still occasionally darken the door of a church. But he had seen that there was art in those accursed practices, the art of healing. Not the science, the art! And that insight is what had brought Rivers to the forefront of modern Western psychiatry. She had understood that almost instinctively. The first time she heard about it, she felt quite moved. A dry, factual account in a professional journal had touched her deeply.

Reymaker had not taken to it as easily, even though he and Rivers knew each other. Had met at some or other conference. They were perhaps even friends; she had bargained on them being more than just passing acquaintances. Reymaker had, after all, attended Rivers's Fitzpatrick lecture in

38

London, even though he was fairly sceptical of his colleague's "new approach" to the treatment of soldiers' hysterical episodes. But the two of them, she and her boss, had debated the subject often enough so that when she had her plans in order, there was little need for a preamble. She'd cut to the chase: "You have contact with Dr Rivers?" And then, "I was wondering whether you could perhaps arrange a position for me." When his eyebrow arched, she quickly added: "The experience could mean something for the practice in the long run."

His mouth fell open, and then he looked down sullenly at the papers on his desk. "I see," he grumbled, "your burning ambition."

Oh, old Reymaker! His irritability did not surprise her, and hadn't for years. Their skirmishes had become a form of familiarity. "No, this is about Rivers," she'd said emphatically, "I mean, his method." Ensuring that her voice remained at an even pitch, she went on, "It's new, not so? You said so yourself. And more than that, the whole phenomenon ... indeed ..." She did not spell it out; it was not necessary to say the word, the word that the war had given to the world. Even in the Netherlands, where people continued to tend their little city gardens, and also in their clinic in Dordrecht where words like neurasthenia, dementia and idiotism were put to bed under pure white sheets daily, even there the mere mention of the word brought a shiver down the spine: shellshock.

Shellshock. Shellshock hospital. Soldiers who have been shot of all sense, rendered mute, robbed of memory, of muscular control; bodies beset by spasms of an otherworldly horror, soldiers who desired nothing more than death.

It is however where she wanted to go. No, "wanted" is not the word. She had thought about this determination of hers on the boat coming over, and if she were to be honest, she was probably driven here by an inner strength of which she was totally unaware. Or rather, unaware then, because that strength had manifested earlier in her life. It was more than likely the same vigour that had spurred her on when she was only eighteen to go off and study in a foreign country, a foreign culture, virtually woman alone, eventually to get a post at Reymaker Psychiatrie.

It was he, Reymaker, who'd come specially to recruit her during her final practical year at Wilhelmina House in Amsterdam, by which time she already had years of training behind her. He wanted none other than the best psychiatry student to assist him in his clinic in Dordrecht. The most reliable, is what he was actually after, she thought bitterly at times in later years, although bitterness is an emotion she has guarded against her whole life.

The one who would complain least, that is what he wanted.

But what he did not know then, and what her lecturers didn't suspect either, was that her diligence was the result of her passion. Or volatility. But call it what you wish, she still believes, sitting here under Hurst's cool appraising gaze, that she conveys her opinion in a civil manner. She is direct, she can take strong positions, but she is decent. Decent in an Afrikaans way? Oh well, it's not important, she then decides. For all practical purposes, she is Dutch.

She therefore does not bother to correct Hurst. "In the Netherlands," she says, "psychiatric nursing care is primarily the domain of women." That's the simple truth, although not just any woman gets awarded the yellow cross. They must be middle class, seeing that this class of woman is considered the standard-bearer of the founding values of a healthy society. Psychiatric patients are seen as people who have strayed from these values and should thus be brought back to the path of righteousness. She thinks again of the farming women she'd seen at the roadside and says: "Here, things are possibly different, but we must ... I must accept that the war has turned everything upside down."

"No, we also have many women here, as you will soon realise. But not many foreigners. I assume people help in their own countries, but yes, in neutral countries it is another matter altogether. You could just as well have gone to work in Germany."

Strange that the issue of where she was going to work had come up for discussion when she'd sounded out Reymaker.

He'd sat staring at his beloved cat, and gave the question a wide berth. "Against England I have no objection. On the contrary. I am talking about the idea of England." He had tilted his head sideways so that one of those charcoal pupils could pin her down.

The idea of England? She wanted to let that phrase simply drift along the stream of words, a description that was little more than a formality, but it had stuck. She immediately wanted to dismiss this vague irritation, but failed. The idea

of England? What had it meant to her? As she quickly re-
flected, some impressions fluttered through her mind like
startled nocturnal birds: keening bagpipes playing "God Save
the King", a bell tent glowing like a lantern in a black, black
night, a lantern jerking and swinging as if dangling from a
wagon. The onset of anxiety was immediate, and she could
recall nothing other than this tumult of images. Only later,
when she'd probably already returned to her room, did the
realisation dawn on her that England would always be only
that to her, that was the problem. Always back to that same
scene. A scene with its own background music, its own lighting, its own words; the choreography of that macabre dance
for ever etched into her mind.

But that realisation only came to her later. Right then,
there, in that office, Reymaker spoke again: "And Rivers?
What you know and admire about him is what I have told
you. I tend to think he takes his admiration for the primitive
a bit too far, that I have told you ad nauseam. That wild, un-
tamed man!" Reymaker pushed a belly laugh into the cat's
face, but abruptly grew more sombre, as if he suddenly realised that he was offending the little statue. "He takes things
too far," he continued thoughtfully. "But yes, he gets results,
not so?" He reached a pale hand towards the cat and carefully
stroked the tail that was curled neatly – so characteristically
feline – around the feet. He glanced at her again from behind
the statue. "It's the war, isn't it?" he said. "You're drawn to
the war."

She looked at him quietly. Weighed his words, her fingertips
resting lightly on the back of the chair. Was it the war? She

looked at her boss on his throne, flanked by his statue of the goddess of wisdom. Anyone else would have burst out laughing at the eccentric old man, but she has learnt to take such caricatures in her stride. To tell the truth, she found it quite reassuring. It would have been harder if he'd been someone you had to take seriously. But is it the war that entices her? And if so, why?

No, she then decided. She chose this profession to be a healer; her life's journey had led to those wounds that lie deepest and are slowest to heal, the wounds to the soul. And she is going to England because there are wards crowded with people whose souls have become caverns filled with flying shrapnel. "It is the people in the war that draw me," she said.

Reymaker gazed at her and then riffled through some papers on his desk. "Oh, well, then," he mumbled. She just needed to arrange a temporary replacement; he helped her to get a concession to travel and a post at one of Rivers's hospitals.

Not at Rivers's actual hospital, the Craiglockhart War Hospital in Edinburgh, but at the Seale-Hayne Hospital in Devon. "There's a chap doing equally good work down there. Rivers seems to think he is on the right track, so that can mean only one thing. His name is Hurst."

And here she sits, across from Doctor Arthur Hurst. Major Hurst. A British soldier, in uniform. It is not a run-of-the mill situation. Certainly not for her. But this is exactly where her life choice, her career choice, was destined to lead her.

She could have spent her life running away from what she is, from what she had become in South Africa. But long ago she had already decided that there is only one way to survive, and that is in direct confrontation with the very thing that would continue to knock at her front door. But one's not compelled to take such a sombre view, because, after all, her life was also saved there, in South Africa, and she'd simply decided to continue that sort of rescue work; the healing that she'd received at the hands of Tiisetso and Mamello in that cave is what she would promote. That's how Rivers came into the picture. She would not give in to the wish to see someone suffer as she had suffered. The desire is still there at times. But that is not a foundation on which to build a life.

Hurst speaks again, and she listens with intense concentration. "But your interest in psychiatry, that is not necessarily an obvious choice?" he says.

That is not a surprise. She's already had to answer that question a few times. In nursing college. Often. After that, Reymaker had asked … But long before that, she'd had to clarify it for herself. These are the facts she sits with: She was the daughter of a sharecropper, a child of the concentration camps. Well, perhaps not a child, but the fact remains that by any standards her education was defective. How did it come to be that someone with her background landed up in psychiatric nursing?

She has a few stock responses, but this time, before Hurst, she's decided to evade the question entirely. "Yes, probably not," she says, "but I came for professional reasons." He looks down at his hand stretched out on the desk, and then again at her. She continues: "For a while, it must have been about ten years ago, women were actively recruited for psychiatric nursing in the Netherlands. Specifically, virtuous middle-class women." She gives an ironic chuckle, a studied gesture. "This sort of nursing is premised on the reintegration of patients into the community. The first priority was to inculcate good civic values, and the Dutch authorities thought middle-class women were ideally suited to the task of bringing lost sheep back into the fold."

"So that's how you landed in your profession – by chance?"

He has not accepted her explanation at face value after all. "No," she says, "not by chance." He was not going to let her get away with it. "Luck was also on my side." Briefly pausing, she continues: "There were people, though, who inflenced me, people who helped me make the decision. They also made it possible for me, in a practical way."

"And now you are here. I suppose that was also not by chance?"

She senses that he is not satisfied with her vagueness. Careful, now.

"No, also not." Again that smile. "Seems to me I am rather impressionable … It was your colleague, Dr Rivers. I'd heard of his work; he and my employer in the Netherlands are …" – are they friends? – "are in close contact and I wanted to, on behalf of our practice, gain some experience in his type of healing."

He lightly nods his head: "And I assume in the Netherlands shellshock does not exist? I see. Yes, that makes sense. Or do you know what shellshock is? Have you seen it?"

Not in the Dutch practice, no. She remembers the woman in the Winburg camp who took to eating grass in the corrugated-iron pound where they sent those driven mad by grief

45

to die; she thinks back to the time when she was bereft of all language and reason, proceeding in a cortège of women dressed in black on the road to her own damnation. Her answer is muted: "When I saw it," she says, "the world did not yet have a name for it."

He looks at her attentively before continuing: "Do you know what we are expected to do here? Officially. Do you?"

She does not answer; looks at him blankly, her thoughts still with the swishing of the black silk dresses, like wind rustling through the veld. Shellshock. Is that the name of the thing she has in mind?

"We are the guardians of the nation's morale," he says, and the way his lower lip drops the words makes her suspect a degree of bitterness. "The nation's morale in a time of war. It largely comes down to ensuring that our soldiers are healthy enough to fight. Mentally sound. We need to confirm that these soldiers, our patients, are in the first instance genuinely ill and are not just malingering because they are too scared to continue fighting. Too scared to die. Our task therefore is to get them back into the trenches as quickly as possible."

He looks at her blankly. She is now convinced of his irony. He had ridiculed his official task with great delicacy, or rather with expertly masked cynicism. She is dead certain of having drawn the right conclusion. She therefore risks saying: "I assume, Dr Hurst," – mindful to strike a cautious note – "I assume that in this hospital the welfare of the patient is your first consideration."

Again his mouth twists wryly, and she notices a faint flush

on his cheeks. "We are going to try our best to heal them. And when they are well they can return to society." He lifts his head, and she sees the eyes shining in their sockets as he then says: "And unfortunately our society presently finds itself in a state of war."

She gets the gist of what he is saying. She does not have to answer him. For these men, war is currently the only mode of existence. Normal life is war. It is the only sanctuary. She wants to say what she had intended to say, something about aspects of Rivers's work that she often thought about and more or less understood.

She hears herself saying something else, though: "I think part of the problem is that people think of themselves as being the war and nothing else. The irony is that you have to untangle them from the war in order for them to be ensnared again."

"Or bolster them psychologically to the point where they maintain a distinction between themselves and the war."

It's as if his words are slowly moving towards her through thick mud; one by one, they reach her. "And so you are not your war?" She almost takes fright as the words line up before her. Inside her, etching into her. She has never expressed it that clearly to herself, even though it has been her life's work. Dealing with catharsis, with closure, the winding-up of her war.

You are not your war.

"Exactly," he says and gets up. "But to make that distinction ... I'm telling you, it's often dreadfully difficult. Let me show you what we are dealing with here."

Chapter 6

If I sit up, I can see out of the cave. Not for long, though, because something starts pressing against my temples with such force that my head wants to burst. I lie down again, even though it's easier to keep my thoughts at bay when I'm looking out at something, or at least if I can see the sun shining. At night it's different. It takes a long time to fall asleep, and I just lie there with my eyes open, staring into darkness. I hear birds, the jackal. At times, people calling. From afar. It is then that I am especially fearful that someone will find this cave. It's as if the actual thing I fear is somewhere out there, and not inside this cave. I don't know why I feel this, but there is something out there.

Underneath the cloth wrapped around my head is a hard, husk-like thing. I feel the tautness against my scalp. But I have to keep my head very still, as it hurts when I move. There is also something between my legs. Stuff. I've been able to wiggle my fingers downwards, to feel around. Something grassy has been pushed in there, fastened to my hips with some kind of cloth or bandage. I'm too scared to touch it. I'm actually too scared to think what it might be or why it is there at all. My legs I keep straight and still. I just lie like this with my head on the sack and look up at the paintings above me, and when I close my eyes I can still see the animals overlayed with one another, apparently moving.

I still cannot recall clearly how I came to be here, or what happened to me. My head hurts too much from thinking.

I can remember everything up to the camp; my thoughts can only go back that far. Then my memories hang like dust between the tents, between the coughing and keening and moaning. Then they blow away again. Like breath. Away. I also remember the slaughter of the sheep. That's all I can think of, but I don't remember whether it was in the camp or not. It's that thought that frightens me most. There is also a man's face.

That is why I am sometimes happy to see Tiisetso, even though I still don't know what he wants to do with me. There is also a woman present. I don't know if it is his wife, she is much older than him, pitch-black with age. But she is the one who looks after me. She feeds me *motôho*. It wasn't even necessary for me to see what it was in order to recognise it. I know that sour, floury taste. She also gives me cold water that she scoops with a tin mug from a clay pot. The water with the bitter taste of leaves.

She is dressed decently, the woman that is here with Tiisetso. With a long whitish dress that buttons to the collar, and a headscarf. Mamello is her name. She speaks Afrikaans, and she talks to me even though I'm still unable to speak. And the bit of Sotho I know won't help much. She keeps telling me that if I need to pass water I must call her. The stuff against my skull and between my legs is medicine that

Tiisetso makes, he is a *ngaka*, a herbalist. That is what she says. Yes, he wears those bracelets around his wrists, I've seen those before. Copper and colourful beads and animal skins.

Mamello talks more than Tiisetso. I want to ask her what they're going to do to me. They don't have guns, that I can see.

She makes a fire, packs kindling and dung cakes, keeping her head away from the smoke.

When he greets, Tiisetso says *kgotso*. Peace. Good for him, greeting like that in the middle of this war. At least he is not part of Olof Bergh's Scouts, burning down farms and killing chickens. Pestilential scum. Also, Tiisetso doesn't have a hat like the ones that the Scouts wear. Neither a gun nor a hat. If only he'd tell me what happened, why I am lying here.

Perhaps I don't want to know everything. I don't want him to tell me what happened here between my legs. But Tiisetso also won't tell me everything. I know he won't, they're like that, these people. Don't look you in the eye, always talking in circles.

I will not move, Tiisetso, I don't feel well, but you must talk. I want to know. I know it is very bad, because it's not only pain that I feel, not only that, there is something very seriously wrong with me.

Tiisetso can probably see what I want, because he is talking to me. He says he can only tell me what he sees, but what does that mean? Shortly afterwards he tells me that he found me like this, but how this came about only I can know. That is what he says. He says I must say myself what happened. He found me like this, and it seems that that is all he wants to say. He says if we could find out what happened to me, we could

50

get medicine for the whole country. The whole country is dying of this disease, he says.

I don't know what he is talking about. It makes me very tired. How did he find me? He must talk straight, not in a roundabout way. I don't know if I understand what he is saying.

He says I, who was dead, was there. He found me there. I was there but I was also not there. I had gone to the other side. As he says that, he gestures with his hand towards the hill. He said I came back and then he found me there in the veld, in the grass. He said I was broken. Shattered. He says it is a great pity, but it's true. That is how this creature speaks. I don't have the strength for it. Rather let Mamello come, she'll be able to explain this nonsense to me.

But I know what he means with his gestures towards the hill. I know. And I also know why I constantly see the sheep being slaughtered. But that face next to the sheep, that is the worst.

Fortunately, Mamello is also here now. She blows on the fire, gently and evenly. When she breathes out, it is like wind moving over the fire. Smoke blows over me. When she speaks, like now, it feels as if her voice comes with the smoke, because her voice comes and goes. She says it's true that I lay there. On the flat earth, halfway between the tents and the stream where they wash the laundry, that is where I lay. The wagon that carried the dead into town each morning dropped me there. She said I was broken. Very badly broken. She says that they, the people of the camp, sent me away with the dead because I was so broken.

Now I know. Tiisetso is one of those who walk around the tents every day. Sometimes he gets fresh milk, and sometimes meat. Or potatoes. Flour can be obtained if you know the people in the camp who distribute the food. That is what Mamello says. And she says I was very badly broken.

As she spoke, I went and lay on my back. Above me, animals and little men with their sticks. She probably thought I'd fallen asleep, but I hadn't. I was thinking and trying to remember. I can see something of what she described, and it feels as if it's stirring inside me. Something within, scraping to and fro, like branches in the wind. They think I am sleeping, those two blacks, but I am not sleeping.

Mamello starts to sing. Then Tiisetso too. They do that. Their voices go round and round and up and down. It goes on and on. It's like smoke billowing over me, their singing. I want to tell them that my name is Ntauleng; that is what our nursemaid called me.

Chapter 7

"Come," Hurst says, putting his pen down on the writing desk, "let me show you what we have to contend with here."

She hesitates, staring half dazed through the window behind him, aware of the sudden light, and an expectant curiosity in herself, almost a feeling of excitement, after the mounting unease of her conversation with Hurst. Yes, she realises, it was not a comfortable conversation. It's not as if Hurst has a prickly personality, quite the contrary. It's just … she can't quite put a finger on it now.

Hurst takes long, energetic strides across the room, yanks open the door. "As I explained earlier, our primary interest here is fear and the effort to master it."

For a moment she is amused by the contrast between the vigour of his movements and the serenity of his face, but then hurries to exit with him. He is not tall, she now realises; perhaps shorter even than she is.

"You might just as easily say we're working with bravery," he continues as she falls into step beside him, "with the expectation that this creates, and the consequent setbacks too. There are still those in the army and outside who think we're seeing to misfits, those who are weak in spirit, susceptible to these breakdowns. But the fact is that most of our patients are officers. You might ascribe that to class, that they would naturally receive more attention and sympathy from the authorities, but the main reason is that officers in particular don't dare show their emotions. They are the men who simply have to dismiss their fear. And here you see the whole caboodle: ataxic and tabetic gait, contractions and anaesthesia of the face, muscle spasms, knee and ankle jerks, paraplegia, hyperthyroidism, amnesia, alexia, aphasia, and then all the other common symptoms that you'd know from the clinical practice."

They walk down a long, shadowy hall with a gleaming polished floor. She is aware of her dress flapping against her legs, of the thudding of Hurst's heavy boots. They walk through a strange, ethereal shimmering of darkness and light – past open doors where electric beams fall almost blindingly bright across the dark passageway. As if she and Hurst have sheathed themselves in a thin membrane of modern knowledge, the latest scientific terms, a delicate net of words, and in this bright bubble they are adrift on an ancient sea, surrounded by convulsing bodies, writhing limbs, and eyes that plop glassily through the porous surface of antediluvian mud and slime. Gradually, something of the primordial soup starts seeping into their clarity, pushing through the molecules of the membrane and forcing open cracks for figures, faces and sounds to penetrate. Along with Hurst's descriptions there is also another voice in her head, one of the old voices that still visit her sometimes, that of Dr Molesworth in a dark carriage en route to Bloemfontein: "What is it that you saw,

Perry?"And while Hurst's voice charts the new terrain for her, her attention is constantly diverted along these other, older roads – the roads she walked to get here, to this hospital. "It's the war, isn't it?" she hears Reymaker speaking, and sees his pale wrinkled finger stroking his cat's tail. "You are not your war," she wants to shout at him; she wants to see him shutting his eyes and recoiling, but Hurst has suddenly come to a standstill.

It was not unexpected; she was just lost in thought. Hurst had in fact been stopping all along to explain things. She'd noticed, for example, that he pauses before descending a flight of stairs, or when they're out of earshot of the staff they periodically encounter in the hallways. "Shellshock is a misleading term," he then says. "Initially, the medical fraternity thought it was nerve damage due to explosions. No, correction, initially they thought it was the scheming of cowards trying to escape the front. So they were treated pretty roughly. Solitary confinement. Punishment. You can imagine what it entailed. Electric shock. Emotional manipulation. But these days we know that many of the soldiers, the ones you see here, haven't even been near a bomb, and that's why we speak of 'battle fatigue' rather than 'shellshock'. In many cases, it's rather the ceaseless exposure to fear, tension, and simply days and weeks and months of waiting in a trench that causes the damage."

They walk into halls, past beds with drab blankets, white sheets and grey faces. Some of the patients don't even see them, staring at the ceiling instead, or out of a window. The nurses whom they come across in the wards are generally so busy that they don't look up. Hurst occasionally bends down next to a bed to speak to a patient; sometimes he elicits a smile, a few words, but mostly just an anxious, bewildered stare. Sometimes Susan wants to ask something, comment, but everything she wants to say feels inadequate. It's as if she's lost her clinical distance and can only respond with personal impressions or emotional statements.

After Hurst has pulled shut the umpteenth door behind them, she wants to grasp the opportunity before the next one to say something that has nothing to do with her. She raises a hand towards him to draw his attention, but just then the door opens on the opposite end of the hallway and a nurse stands in the opening, her expression inscrutable. Susan swallows, her throat dry. She literally swallows her words, and her hand slowly drops to her side. Above the nurse's head, in that fraction of a second before the door closed behind her again, she'd seen a body recoiling upwards from a bed, as if the sheets were a white-hot flame – that was a human being.

The door clicks shut, and Susan and the woman face each other in silence. That was a human being, Susan thinks, and feels the delayed shock of adrenalin pricking her fingertips. She hears Hurst speak from behind. "Anne," Hurst says to the nurse, "won't you show Nurse Susan Nell the ropes?"

The woman opposite her, Anne, her blue eyes, her whole face is immobile, only her mouth moves when she speaks, and then with an almost cynical slant to the full bottom lip. She is Anne Maxwell, apparently one of the senior nurses in the hospital, but exactly where she fits into the hierarchy is not clear. She seems to be aware of the arrival of the "Dutch-woman", but she listens to Hurst's brief introduction with a deadpan look, almost absent, similar to that of hospital staff when taking a pulse reading. She watches Hurst as he walks away, and once he is out of earshot, she addresses his receding back: "What has he already shown you? One of his miracles?"

It is a flat, somewhat bored tone, but the blue eyes flash at Susan and then glare pointedly to where Hurst has disappeared around a corner. Susan suspects that the woman is parodying the typically strict matron. She is not certain how to react to it. Is Anne Maxwell mocking Hurst? She ignores Anne's sideways glance and says softly: "The people I've seen looked pretty haggard."

Anne immediately starts to stride ahead. "Come," she says, "come, let me show you." Susan falls into step with her, and with her gaze still fixed ahead she says: "Those who are healed, miraculously healed, or on the verge of improvement, you will see in the library, or in the music room, or strolling in the garden."

Susan is unsure of the exact import of the woman's words. Miraculous ... is she being sarcastic? It is merely a passing thought, though, because what really occupies her mind is what she had fleetingly seen behind that door. She lengthens her stride so as to walk just ahead of Anne Maxwell, looks over her shoulder, and asks, "What was that in the ward behind us, where you've just come from?"

Anne's eyes swivel towards her and then back again, a fleeting gesture, meaning what exactly? Was it a confirmation? A warning? But before Susan can even ask, Anne speaks. "Percy Meek," she says, and then: "Not yet ready for the library or a stroll in the garden, would you agree?" Susan stares at her. What is the woman talking about? Anne continues undeterred: "You should have seen him when he was admitted." She bangs the door open with her left hand and they enter a room with a long table and chairs; emanating from somewhere are kitchen sounds and the smell of food being steamed. "The staff dining room," says Anne, standing at the head of the table, folding her hands in front of her chest and continuing without a pause: "He thought he was still in a trench when he got here, lying prostrate and dodging bombs, his pupils as large as saucers." She looks Susan squarely in the eye for the first time, and then Susan notices it: her irises have a navy, almost purple edge. And below those eyes, the lips scarcely seem to move as they shoot out volleys of words: "There in his bed, totally spastic, he sweated like a horse, his pulse a hundred and forty, and his head, trunk, legs, everything, shaking. He sees ghosts," she says, "the ghosts of the Germans he brought down with his bayonet. They're coming for him, he hears their bullets smashing down next to him, they're coming for him."

Susan still does not know how to react. Beneath Anne's severe exterior, her expressionless face and the monotone of her description, a keen intelligence shines through; the account even sounds rehearsed, and the mouth, Susan notices, yes, the mouth is always just a hair's breadth away from a smile.

Susan begins to suspect a playful irony, but again Anne continues before she can say anything. This time, though, she has a question: "But why did you come and work here? Why not in a general hospital? That's where the staff shortages are. To treat trench foot, or the thousands of cases of venereal disease. Not to mention those who've been blown to bits. Shell-shock is but a drop in the ocean."

The woman is pulling her leg, no doubt about it. Susan drops her defences, and the words jump right out of her mouth. "Thousands of cases ... what do you mean?"

"Oh, it's common ..." Anne begins, but Susan's spontaneous response is immediately overcome by a sombre suspicion that she has said something untoward, something improper, that she has exposed herself. "I'm sorry," she backtracks, alarmed, "I didn't answer your question." She examines Anne's face to gauge the effect of her words, but the blue irises with the dark rim betray nothing. "I was trained as a psychiatric nurse," she then says, her voice strong, the delivery firm.

This time Anne raises an eyebrow. "Oh, really?" she says. "Do you have that type of specialisation in the Netherlands?" She doesn't seem to want a response, because the next sentence is already flowing as unhurriedly as the rest: "Iron restraint, you were taught that, I can see. And that's good enough for this place. But what am I talking about, here they require only the best, because if you make an error with one of these men's diagnoses, the firing squad could be his fate. Rat-a-tat-tat. Not something that'll happen if you incorrectly diagnose foot rot, right? So, chin up and smile, you're at the forefront of military medical science." Iron restraint? That is what she thinks about as she walks down the hallway next to Anne. Susan notices that she takes long, easy strides, and for a while she enjoys walking in step with her; a sort of military camaraderie in their synchronised paces, a bravado even, but then it seems silly to Susan and she consciously changes her stride.

59

Still, there was something in this fleeting, inconsequential experience that has left her with a tingling sensation, and then she dares, also because Anne's spirited irreverence has made it possible, she dares to give up some of that alleged restraint. "Do they also shoot those with venereal diseases?" she asks.

"What?" Anne barks melodramatically, but still without the trace of a smile. "Perhaps where you come from, but here we're civilised."

It jolts through Susan. Where she comes from? Yes! That's in fact what she has in mind, Susan realises. For a while now, that's what she's wanted to say. While Anne was speaking, heaven knows for how long, an old image came to mind, it was in her head, here, in the passage, and back there, in the kitchen, and it was something that Anne had said that gave rise to this thing, this image from her youth. It was in Cape Town, yes, that's where she'd seen it, it was one of the English soldiers, a captain, who had brazenly walked down Adderley Street with a prostitute on each arm, utterly at ease, as if he … as if he … but it's not that either, no, not that, it's actually just the simple fact that she'd lived in Cape Town for a while and that, practically speaking, she hailed from there. For some or other reason she did not tell Hurst, did not want to tell him, but now in this hospital hallway, and to a woman she has known for barely more than five minutes, here she wants to say where she comes from. "In Cape Town, once …" she begins, then holds her breath.

"Cape Town? Have you been there?" Anne enquires above the click-clack of her shoes.

Susan slowly exhales. "That's where I actually come from," she says. "Before the Netherlands. That is where I grew up."

Goodness, that was easy, she thought. Why, then, was it so difficult for me before? No, probably not difficult, but still, with Hurst it was an issue, a kind of obstacle, and this thing about her origin is what gave the conversation with Hurst an underlying awkwardness, like an unwanted touch, like fingers that … she shudders, shakes her head to banish the thought.

Only then does Susan realise that Anne has come to a halt, and that she's walked five steps or so ahead without her. She stops immediately and turns around to her colleague, and it strikes her that Anne has the ideal face for this era and this place, for this war, with those purple-haloed eyes and that steely mouth. "Then you're a woman who has come a long way," Anne says. "You can tell me more than I can tell you." She starts walking again, this time with a gaze firmly fixed on Susan.

Chapter 8

Lebitso la ka ke Ntauleng.

I have spoken! I have told Mamello what my name is. Ntauleng. I can speak again! And she clapped her hands in gratitude and bent down and laughed and cried lilililili and quickly ran down the hill to call Tiisetso. He came and stood in the cave with his knobkerrie held high and said: *Kêna ka kgotso, Ntauleng.* Come inside in peace, Ntauleng. I think he means that I should come inside from wherever I have been. Mamello starts fussing with the calabash, but Tiisetso just stands there staring at me, the handle of his knobkerrie held next to his ear. Perhaps he knows about the nights, how I lie awake in the dark, strangled by fear and struggling to breathe, and that I am always listening, to every little sound. Sometimes I hear a horse's teeth against a bit, or a stamping hoof, then something wing-like passes over me, or a crowd of women with black dresses and big black hoods walk slowly through the veld and the dresses touch one other with a scraping sound, and from their bodies comes the smell of dassie droppings, the excrement fermenting in crevices, and from the corners of the women's mouths bitterness drips down the jagged rock.

They started singing, Tiisetso with a high voice for a man, and Mamello's also high, but flatter, as smooth and flat as the rock where they slaughter. And while they sang, I said the words that came into my head, just because I could speak again, I said them. Just because I could speak again.

Whore! I'd said. Whore! And again: Whore! I heard myself say it, the word just came out. It's actually the only word that came out. The two black people sang, stood next to each other and sang with their bodies swaying to and fro as if they were being tugged by the wind, and I lay there and it felt as if I were being bled dry like a sheep with a slit throat.

Now I know where the word comes from. The man who caught me like a sheep between the tents and pulled me by my leg to the place of slaughter while I kicked and kicked and kicked. He said it. He said it to me. That is what I am. Look, I throw her down onto the bed, and those who fornicate with her – look, I am the one who inspects kidneys and hearts, who sticks my hand into innards and rips them from the carcass – cast her into the outer darkness, feed her to the dogs whose jaws work lewdly throughout the night.

The blacks sing, but it is of no help, it takes nothing away. They can do with me what they wish. I am worthless.

The Lord will spit me out of His mouth. Whore is my name! And from His mouth came a sharp two-edged sword: and His countenance was as the sun that shineth in her strength, as the sun that shineth in her strength.

Chapter 9

The woman dithers around at the door as if she were looking for something far away. What could it be, a pet that has
slipped past her feet? Mrs Simms.

It's a kind of dance, Susan thinks. Like a small ritual that
needs to be completed before the woman can take notice of
whoever has knocked on the door.

Jacobs had dropped her off here and introduced her to
her landlady. Mrs Simms has been living alone since her husband's death and therefore has a spare room that she rents
out occasionally. A small shrivelled face, a nodding head, a
condescending little laugh. She hardly acknowledges Jacobs;
he laughs sheepishly before the woman shuts the door in his
face and then worms her way in front of the surprised Susan
to show her to her room.

Afterwards they sit in the living room, Mrs Simms in the
brown chair, Susan in the blue. As it has to be, Susan realises.
The old woman looks at her with a satisfied smile, and not
without the condescension evident from the outset, as if this
person had just delivered evidence of some or other comical
human failing.

"Correct me if I am wrong, my dear," she says. "You come

from the Netherlands and you are going to work at that hospital." She has a continual smile on her face.

Ah, there it is again, the question regarding her origin. Susan feels she has figured out the lay of the land by now. In the Netherlands she does not mince her words, on principle, if someone asks, but here, she now knows with certainty, something has shifted.

She is still unsure why it had happened, but it probably has something to do with what Reymaker referred to as "the idea of England". "My issue is not with the idea of England ..."

The idea of England? It has something to do with that. It's even got something to do with the fact that Mrs Simms in her absolute Britishness, in her eccentricity, seems vaguely familiar to her, that there is something in her mystifying haughtiness that she instinctively understands. Oh, and of course this country and its people, its history, have obvious connotations for her, but those are things she has left behind and does not allow to control her life. She therefore states quickly, adamantly, in the face of her landlady's all-knowing gaze: "South Africa. I actually come from South Africa. But I have been working in the Netherlands for the past sixteen years."

Mrs Simms's face brightens. She turns her head as if she wants her smile to be admired from all sides. "South Africa? You don't say!" For a moment or so she sits there, as if enraptured. Susan leans forward with a slight frown between her eyes. And then Mrs Simms's thoughts find their footing again and she begins to talk with her right hand tugging at her chest, as if she were literally making the stream of words enter the light of day. "Luckily we have another war to concern ourselves with now, not so," she says. "And what a mess it is. What a miserable mess. And this time your people are fighting there together with us. That's how things go these days. One moment they're fighting tooth and nail, and the next they're falling about each other's necks.

"I do wonder what my mother would have made of it. You know, she was only twelve when she was made to milk the cows. Every morning at four o'clock. Milking time. A respectable woman, my mother was. My father was an orphan, and the one advantage of being in the orphanage was that he learnt a trade. A blacksmith is what he was, and thanks to him I have this house. My husband worked on the railways all those years, and with his salary …" she flaps her hand in a throwaway gesture. "You know how it goes. What I have I inherited from my parents. Do you have any family there?"

Does she have any family there? Where? In her fatherland or in the trenches?

But the question does not actually mean anything, she reminds herself. Why should she take it to heart? These are the standard pleasantries of a kindly woman who is starved of company. Besides, this flood of personal information from a complete stranger is not strange, especially if you work in a psychiatric clinic. But it feels as if all questions here in England regarding her origins are charged with meaning, or is this only since her meeting with Hurst? Or the moment she saw her first patients? But there is something, something that is allowing things to merge that she'd always managed to keep apart in the past. For a long time, it has hardly ever been necessary for her to think of South Africa as her country.

And now the most innocent question seems loaded. Does she still have family there? In the Netherlands, she seldom thinks of it that way. Since Aunt Marie's death, Jack Perry is essentially her only contact with her past. In almost every respect, the country has left her bereft. She must not, oh, Lord, why does she think about it now, but then the thought is there, irrevocably so: There is a grave with her name on the tombstone, a register with her death certificate. It was supposed to end there. And that is where she wants it to end.

But does she have anyone left there? From her first life she has nothing at all. Not even the dinner service with the blue floral pattern. Just a few memories that would mean nothing to outsiders. Her mother fixing her father's collar before he places his shoe in the stirrup and swings his right leg over the horse. An enamel mug dangling from the saddle. Ma touching Pa's calf one last time, his trousers against the horse's trembling flank, but in fact just wanting to hide under the bonnet, not wanting to show how afraid she was of the endless bare veld with its riders and smoke and dust, and of what would come after the riders left, once the smoke had blown away and the dust had settled. That is at least something, she thinks. At least I have that.

Mrs Simms looks at her expectantly, and Susan, alarmed, tries to remember the thread of the conversation, but struggles to disentangle her thoughts from those old memories. She looks down at her hands, bends her fingers so that her nails dig sharply into her thighs, and only then, when the physical prickling is felt, does she remember the woman's question. "Yes," she says then, stumbling over her words at first, but quickly regaining her composure, "or not really, but the fact that I am here and can work here, here in your country, I really have the goodness of other people to thank for that."

"You mean you have family here?"

"No, what I mean is that in Cape Town, where I come from …" She will also have to tell Hurst at some point! "I received money that enabled me to go and study in the Netherlands. There I qualified as a psychiatric nurse, and now I am here."

"So far from home and hearth?"

Should she state candidly that she has nobody, that her parents died in the war, and that her only brother did too? That there was no other family? Should she talk about that now?

Mrs Simms's smile has finally disappeared, she sees, and her mouth is now shaped into a little beak, an inquisitive bow, ready to say "oh" or "poor thing" or to make some other meaningless sound of an old person. "I am used to it by now," Susan says, looking down at her hands, which remain pressed flat against her thighs. Her answer echoes in her head. Used to it? She and Ma sitting on their knees in the freshly dug red soil with the kitchen utensils wrapped in flour sacks, and the three men approaching them through the bluegums. Susan quickly sits forward in her chair; she wants to jump up, she does not know what has come over her. Is it this country? Is it the hospital that is, after all, so different to what she had imagined? She hears Hurst's and her own footsteps down the hallway, she sees a body shaking and twisting as if it were possessed, Anne Maxwell's mouth mimicking the sound of a machine gun and far below them in the unkempt garden two men in uniform strolling about as if that garden were the only thing in creation, as if there was no killing field that they had come from, or a hospital ward to which they had to return, as if everything, this country with its women bursting exuberantly from men's trousers, with its wet green fields and sagging sky, the terrible war itself, as if it were all just a dream.

"Oh, but what kind of life is that?" Mrs Simms cries out. "No wonder you go and sit in that awful old hospital. Oh, well, I have no more kin either. My husband has been gone some nine years, I think? – Yes, that's how long he's been dead. No children, none. Not that it bothers me much. But you are young, it's a different matter altogether."

Susan balls her hands on her thighs, wringing them on her lap. She must try to concentrate on what the woman is saying, she must focus her attention, but it feels as if she's walking through a field of stubble and thousands upon thousands of startled doves have engulfed her in a cacophony of wings, like live grapeshot. She feels the throbbing in her throat. What is going on with her? Impressions, images, memories, things she cannot express are worming their way into a simple conversation with a kind woman ... is worming the word? Yes, that's the word. Everything that is said becomes an allusion about who she is and where she belongs. "You don't like the Seale-Hayne Hospital?" she then says, remembering to smile politely.

The woman just snaps her fingers in the air and turns her head away in annoyance. "Don't pay any attention to me," she says, but when she turns around again, her smile is back. "But do you enjoy it? The work, I mean. Surely one has to be suited for something like that? I'd think that if you survived that war in South Africa, you probably have the constitution for it."

Now she knows what it is. Suddenly it's there, like lighting in the dark. That war! The earth had begun to shift under her when Jacobs showed her that house, and now it's with her again, that war, closer than it has been since she left South Africa. How many of these soldiers weren't there too? Now she knows what it is: In town, somewhere, is the house of General Rundle, the man who'd allowed his men to swarm like ants across the Brandwater valley. She gets up quickly. "You must excuse me ma'am," she says to Mrs Simms, who looks up at her in surprise. "I want to ..." She begins to walk away before completing her sentence. She stands still, then turns around again to the old woman staring at her from the brown chair. "I'm sorry," she says, "I just want to go and quickly do something."

Chapter 10

It's the death whistle I heard, that's what woke me up, not just a dikkop flying upwards. The whistle was blowing for me, and I know what is coming. The mule cart will come, on the road between the tents it will come. One of the Scouts is sitting on the buggy, pricking the thin mules in the rump with a piece of barbed wire. He can come, I'm ready for him, lying here wrapped in the sheet that Ma had pulled off my bed when the Khakis came to fetch us at Bosrand. I will lie swaddled and rocking on the wagon, behind the driver who will be staring from below his wide-brimmed hat at the deeply rutted wagon path on the way into town. Farther behind, Chrissie and Maggie and Alice are singing in the tent, and up ahead the town backs away from that corpse-filled tent, it recoils from that white tent that breathes so heavily through the small slit of the flap.

Far, far behind is the hillside that is so soft with grass, and cloud shadows fall where the hill folds into the earth, and up ahead, closer to the camp but still far away, there are black figures scuttling to and fro, like long-tailed whydahs over the tall grass, somebody on a horse, there is more than one tall man with a blanket around his shoulders, dark spots moving to and fro, coming together and then parting again, probably people, but it could just as easily be black dogs, or calves. There are voices, like a swarm of bees, like the wings of bush doves flushed from fields of wheat, and hooves thundering over fallow earth, and it seems as if the deep growling, pulsing, droning of the song pushes a stain from the shadow on the side of the hill, a stain that grows and grows, the voices swelling and the stain is now a group of people approaching, walking close together, shimmering, rustling dresses and bonnets so large and black that they darken the whole vlei, and in the middle of the heavy dark mass of women I walk, white and almost transparent, like a cutworm in a block of turf, and the black of the dresses drains the blood from me, from the women's bitter mouths and their furious eyes, but Tiisetso walks ahead with a long thin reed like the feeler of a locust, and he lifts his knees slowly and places his feet where the hill tells him to place them, the hill that is soft with grass and even darker from clouds that fold into the flank of the earth, even darker, darker still.

Chapter 11

She pulls the door shut behind her, and without hesitation walks out. She has a vague notion of how to get there; Jacobs's over-enthusiastic tour may yet be of some use. She takes long, determined strides, more to counteract a nervous wobbliness of the knees than out of a sense of purpose. She is no longer wearing her nurse's uniform. The hem of a light summer dress whips around her calves and her knitted hat is pulled down to her ears. She is now her impulsive self, she realises, but what does she want to go and do there? Something within, dissatisfaction, a sort of gnawing unease, must be cleared away. She is not one who avoids this sort of thing; nothing is swept under the carpet. And perhaps there is something … A memory, a person, perhaps. It could be that the general himself is there. What's the chance of that? Jacobs simply said that he'd grown up in that house, not that he is living there now or for that matter has any ties to it. How old would he be now? Perhaps he is no longer even alive? Oh, how stupid she is – she can't believe she is thinking these thoughts. Perhaps fresh air and exercise are all she needs, who knows?

The house is barely ten minutes' walk from Mrs Simms's place. She recognises the stone wall. It is clearly ancient, and the stone is darker than the kraal walls of her childhood, its texture smoother.

She stands next to the wall, touching the stone with her fingertips, pulling grass shoots from a cement seam between the stones. Then she hears a grating noise, and to her left a gate opens. It is an old man in a heavy, baggy jacket. He does not see her, and she stands rooted to the spot. Is it the general? She pinches her bottom lip between her thumb and forefinger. Could it be him? He who had been in charge of those thousands of troops who trekked across the veld like ants, no, like locusts, destroying everything, everything. A tired old man like that?

The man starts moving away, his eyes fixed on something in the distance. He still does not notice her, but she cannot pass up this opportunity. "General?" she says, walking quickly towards him.

Clearly alarmed, he takes a few sideways steps and flails wildly with his arms to keep balance. She grabs him by the elbow to support him, but he pulls away crossly. "Excuse me," he says, "but are you out of your mind …"

"I'm sorry," she says, "I'm sorry." And then uncertainly she adds, "General?"

Gasping, he eyes her suspiciously, warily. "General? What do you mean?"

"Are you not General Rundle?"

"Rundle!" His eyes narrow, his chest heaves four times before he can speak again: "You mean General Sir Leslie Rundle? Huh? Good Lord, my dear child, for all I know he is busy shooting Germans somewhere in France. I could have been his father." It's as if the entire bottom half of his face hangs from two screws positioned where his eyes should be.

Could have been his father ... but is the babbling old man not perhaps his father? "I heard that he grew up in this house," she said.

"I don't know where you get your information, young lady, but this is not at all the house where old Sparkhall Rundle lived, and what was his wife's name again? Ah, I can still see her walking in front of me. You know who I'm talking about, the general's mother. No, it will probably come to me later." His fish-like mouth opens and shuts wordlessly, and then he spits it out: "But, young lady, you are not from here, are you? I am trying to place your accent. You are not a resident, are you?"

"No, you are right, I am not." For a moment she looks away from his watery blue eyes. He can no longer move them, she thinks.

His mouth can still show anger; his voice can still betray him, his throat can still be choked in emotion, but his eyes don't oblige. That's where it starts, she thinks, the eyes. Over his shoulder she sees the neat street, the proud buildings, all the signs of an old established civilisation, a proper town, not just a few little houses thrown together in the dust, or a godforsaken clump of tents, and then she says with cold, considered fury, at once reckless and utterly controlled: "I am a South African."

His mouth falls open ever so slightly; his eyes remain still and bleary, but focused on her. He swallows. "And you are looking for Rundle?" he says, looking down at his shoes and again at her. "I see, I see." Then he glances left down the street, then right, as if he wants to make sure that there is no one close by. "And you've come all this way to see him?"

As quickly as her fury flared up it dies away. "No, not really," she says calmly. "I'm working here, temporarily, and I happened to hear that he grew up here."

"And then you wanted to come and see him. To say what to him, exactly? Excuse me for being so direct, but how old were you in that war?"

"In that war?" She snorts, and quickly brings her fingertips to her mouth. She examines the moist tips before speaking. "Old enough," she says, and she looks the old man squarely in the eye, and sees how his inquisitive eyeballs try to bore into her, searching, and she answers his gaze with all the inner strength she can muster, she has the strength, oh Lord yes, she has the strength. "Old enough," she says again, and feels her mouth twist into a self-deprecatory smirk; then she swings around and walks away.

She was eighteen when she came to her senses in that cave. She was already a woman, but she did not know that yet, not then. When she arrived in that cave with Tiisetso and Mamello it was as a limp and helpless infant, but already branded with the mark of a fallen woman. A war baby. A whore. And they brought her up and sent her into the world. And here she is in another war, and she's come encumbered with that first war. A war baby in a country that she can barely remember, in a concentration camp, then in a cave, then a train … what else? What do you remember of life when you have risen from the dead? Rundle had his headquarters in Senekal, in a house belonging to some farmer – who did it belong to? The Viljoens, perhaps? And where were they, the Viljoens, and how many of them are dead and how many survived, and should one ask them after everything that happened, who would be able to say exactly what happened and what it all meant? What would it mean to this old man if I told him, yes your general sir had his headquarters in Senekal in someone's townhouse and he sent his soldiers out like locusts, like a plague they trekked across the land, one mighty vibrating mass of male flesh, and the whole sky flapped like a tarpaulin in the wind, and fear covered the land like a collapsed tent with its pegs pulled out, and below that tarpaulin are the writhing, kicking, crawling bodies, my God, what does it all mean?

She jerks to a halt and turns around. She looks down the street to see if the old man is still there, but there is nothing. Farther down, there is movement, but where she'd just seen the old man, next to the home of the general, there's just the road, the pavement and a stone wall. There is no sign that anything has happened. And what did happen, after all? Nothing. It doesn't mean a thing. This is another country, another time, and another war. All that matters is that she is strong enough, strong enough to do her work. To help shattered men wrapped in uniforms to get back to their trenches to fight their war.

Chapter 12

But I am alive. I am breathing. I can see. Tiisetso is sitting against the grey sky at the mouth of the cave. The fire still has a small flame. A wisp of smoke, like the mist around the tents when the weather is very cold.

Now I know. Mamello said I must have fallen off the hearse since Tiisetso had found me lying in the grass when he'd gone off at dawn, searching for who knows what in the camp, probably to steal something. Covered in blood. Broken. But he saw that I was still alive, I was not dead, and he brought me here. I don't know how he did it without the Scouts seeing him. They came here and hid me in this cave.

How long have I been lying here? I don't know. In the mornings when I wake up, Tiisetso is sitting in front of the cave. In the evenings when I fall asleep, Mamello is still here. She has packed bushes and branches at the entrance so that people don't notice the fire. I am just waiting for both of them to leave so that I can get myself past the branches to see what is going on, to drag myself, if I have to. I'll discover where they come from, what they're up to.

This morning when I asked Tiisetso what had happened to me, at first he just sat there, and turned his head away, staring at the veld. Then he said, it's this country. There is a big problem. You can almost not go for a walk without stepping on a dead body. He said there are just a few people, very few, who get up again once they've fallen.

Then he kept quiet, his head to the side. At first I thought he'd heard someone coming, but nothing happened. Then he began, *Ba re e ne e re* ... I thought he was going to tell me what had happened, but then I remembered that this is how blacks begin a story, a fable, any made-up tale. Our nursemaid used to do this. *Ba re e ne e re*, they say it was like this that ...

There must be something wrong with Tiisetso, because he told me a long story about this chief of theirs who sent his suffering people a message that their misery would end, but the people believed another man who told them that they would all die.

He mixed Sotho and Afrikaans. He said the chief had sent his son to tell his suffering people that they would die, but they would also rise again. I was listening to what he was saying, I was listening, but there was also something else, something else that I remember. I had to go and find some medicine, that is why I was in the darkness, outside the tents. Alice was dying, and I simply had to, I had to. They sent me; I was the one who had to go.

I don't know why Tiisetso told me the story. Or perhaps I do know, but I don't have the strength to decipher it. And it doesn't bother me. At least I listened to the story, and in a way it was good to hear it. For now, it is enough to stay here in the cave with the little fire and the smoke and the eland leaping over me and Tiisetso playing his *lesiba* and blowing and blowing until the hoarse, stringy sounds collect like a bunch of grass in my chest, there where I feel my heart should have been.

Chapter 13

Who would she be looking for?

It happens every time. As Mrs Simms opens the front door after Susan has knocked, she peers anxiously over her shoulder, as if she is expecting someone else, another visitor who should be somewhere behind her. Susan has wondered whether she expects a prowler perhaps. Once she has peered out, only then does she make eye contact, taking Susan firmly by both elbows and saying emphatically: "Good afternoon, my darling, how are you?" So pointedly that it sounds like a warning to whoever may be within earshot.

The first few times Susan looked around anxiously, but each time there was only the empty street, the grey atmosphere that pressed heavily down on the terraced houses, their corners softened and rounded by age and decades of interminable rain. In the meantime, though, the landlady had turned around and, apparently unperturbed, gone inside the house.

Susan generally arrives at home well before sunset; would actually prefer to stay at the hospital a little longer to help with the usual routines, but is reliant on the official transport that keeps strict office hours. After her welcoming ritual, Mrs Simms lets her in and locks the door carefully behind her, then she usually picks up a newspaper from a table in the entrance hall and presses a wrinkled finger to the headline, saying: "Have you seen this, my dear?"

Mostly she does not wait for an answer, and instead begins to expound on municipal regulations, the fate of some dignitary or other, or the price of flour or strawberries. Never news of the war, never world politics, or anything even vaguely resembling what Susan considers significant. Today's headline is: *The Americans are in town.*

The Americans? Susan sits as usual in the front room, on the edge of the chair with the grey-blue upholstery. Just for a while, so as not to seem rude. She has come to the conclusion that it is perhaps a soldier that Mrs Simms is so nervous about whenever she opens the front door. She developed this suspicion after Jacobs dropped her off and then waited with the engine running for someone to open the door. When Mrs Simms saw Jacobs she swung around immediately, clucked angrily, and gestured dismissively: Go away! Susan turned around in surprise, but Jacobs responded to her questioning look with a shrug and a provocative roar from his engine.

Does the landlady hold something against her own soldiers specifically? People like Jacobs? Susan has begun to wonder what might happen were a German to come knocking. Would Mrs Simms fall about his neck and invite him in and pull out a chair for him in the gloomy kitchen and give him a stiff gin?

But perhaps Mrs Simms's searching gaze is fixed upon something far more commonplace, because once, in response to a headline about a mice plague in town, halfway through her story, in the middle of a sentence, she fell silent and stood lost in thought with her fist before her mouth, her finger crooked like a small church spire.

Then, out of the blue, she began to speak about something else entirely, as if she'd been dwelling on it for days, and at exactly that moment it had welled up irrepressibly: "I told them I don't take any men, no men ..."

Susan was completely taken aback, but Mrs Simms took her by the arm conspiratorially and completed her sentence: "... and then they said to me – when they were still looking for lodgings for you – they told me no it's a woman that's coming, and she is Dutch."

They stood across from each other, these two women, the older one almost beaming at the younger one, and the younger looking away uncomfortably. It was as if the information was meant to be confidential, but Susan could not immediately ascertain why, and what exactly it was meant to signify. She backed away slowly, and sat in one of the chairs, the blue one. She had stepped away carefully so that it would not appear that she was fleeing. And then Mrs Simms's face became businesslike again; she folded the newspaper and put it back on the table, clasped her hands and said: "They know full well I don't give lodgings to men."

Was that all it meant? The simple fact that men were not welcome here? Mrs Simms, this sweet, wily old woman, has an aversion to men? As simple as that! And yet, and yet ... in a very strange way this deduction does not bring peace of mind either, and the more Susan thinks about it, the stranger it seems, perhaps even upsetting. And she does not know why it should bother her, Susan, so much.

It probably has something to do with this habit Mrs Simms has of peering over her shoulder. She simply cannot get rid of the suspicion that the landlady is expecting someone behind her – a man, to be precise.

What is it with these old women? Susan often thought of those two aunts of her youth, all those long afternoons in their Cape Town sitting room, or the sunroom in winter, the women's rambling conversations, the way they dissected people's behaviour, putting it in context, expressing their opinions and concerns. Long afterwards, and only once she'd tried to explain it to someone, did she grasp the humour, the irony, the bonhomie, the play of light and colour in the nurturing company of those women. She looks at the woman who is now totally hidden by the newspaper trembling as if there were a light breeze in the room, the almost die-hard grip of those puffy fingers on the pages. Slowly, a presumption grows into a certainty: She has appropriated this wariness of Mrs Simms; her landlady's fear is actually her own. What she'd picked up was Mrs Simms's fear that this intimacy between women might be threatened. The two of them here in the hallway, she and the De Wet sisters back then in Cape Town, a self-sufficient whole, shielded from the threat of men.

Mrs Simms slaps the newspaper down onto the table between the two chairs. "And now they are here among us," she says, sitting on the chair with the russet upholstery. Her chair.

Susan is startled. Who might she be talking about? Men? The enemy? Then she remembers Mrs Simms's aversion to the hospital – could it be that she has something against the mentally disturbed? How many times has she not complained about the hospital changing the character of the town? Before the war, everyone lived with the assurance that anyone who could be classified as disturbed in any way would be safely and permanently removed from society and held in some or other institution behind bars. Now the streets are teeming with soldiers and every single one is peculiar, every one of them comes from another, mysterious world, each one stands, as it were, with one foot in the grave. Is that what she is talking about?

"Who, Mrs Simms," she asks carefully, "who is among us?"

The older woman's mouth falls open; it's as if the question has hit her in the face like a wet cloth. "The Americans, of course," she says indignantly. "The station was full of them this morning." She grasps the chair's armrests as if wanting to pull herself up, but then continues more calmly: "It's the first time I've seen one in the flesh, you know."

"An American?"

"A black. Do you have blacks in the Netherlands? I have, of course, seen photographs, but up close ..." Mrs Simms's words drift off, and she puts her little tabernacle fist in front of her mouth, her eyes worried, almost anxious.

Blacks? Susan feels a spasm. She looks at her landlady without immediately knowing what to say. What she does know – or rather, what she feels in the pit of her stomach – is that Mrs Simms's comment, her question, touches her personally, as if it were aimed at some intimate personal detail.

But before she can say anything, Mrs Simms sits up and curtly announces that the food is ready.

Susan helps with taking the serving dishes to the table, but neither of them says a word. True, in the Netherlands there is hardly a black face to be seen, and what would happen if she were to run into Tiisetso, for example? Goodness, when last did that name come up? It seems so strange to her that there should be such a thing as the first time you saw a black person. Perhaps that's what sets her apart from Mrs Simms, and, for that matter, from all the Dutch people she knows. She, at least, would not run a mile. But that is not what this is about either. It is as if Mrs Simms ... Could it be? Oh please, now she's really gone mad. It can't possibly be the case that Mrs Simms has been seeing a black person over her shoulder all this time!

Susan watches her landlady furtively. They begin to eat in silence, lost in their own thoughts, and it seems to Susan as if they're wary of each other's opinions. Then Mrs Simms lets her hands fall on either side of her plate, the knife and fork like drumsticks in her fists. "Have you seen them yet?" she says, speaking into the powdery air in front of her. She chews and swallows before tilting her face towards Susan, and explains: "The women commandos in the fields?"

The forkful of bully beef and rice stops halfway to Susan's mouth. She lowers it slowly back onto the plate and wipes her mouth with a serviette. Now she gets it.

Mrs Simms no longer has it in for the blacks, but for the Women's Land Army. What a leap! She is now talking about those women ... those cheerful, defiant women who commandeered the road – oh, they were probably all very young, mere girls. Suddenly Susan is among them again on Jacobs's motorbike, experiencing again that very first sight of them, the shouting from generous moist mouths, the roaring laughter, the preposterousness of it all. "You mean those women in the tight pants?" Susan says. "Is that what you're talking about?"

Mrs Simms flaps her wrist in the air and clucks disapprovingly. "But at least there are those you see in decent dresses and with something proper on the head." She pulls a serving dish towards her, but to Susan it seems as if the bowl itself is inching forward obligingly under that critical gaze. "There are of course people who have much to say about the farming women." With two stubby forefingers she makes scare quotes around "farming". "But let me tell you who has the most to say: men. Men who have neither the backbone to go and fight, nor enough calluses on their hands to plough the fields. Ah, if only I was ten years younger ..." She reflects for a moment, her chin on her wrist. "Kenneth would turn in his grave," she says with a grimace. "My husband has been gone for a good nine years, and you know, although I have many dear memories of the old man, dear Lord, if I wanted to go and buy a piece of ribbon, or a packet of sugar for the house, he first had to come with his bunch of keys to unlock the money drawer. Like a ..." She grasps at the word with her fingers. "I had to beg like a child."

Susan sits dumbstruck in front of this deluge of words. She feels a bit embarrassed for having no response, looks down at her plate and picks up her fork. Could it be ...? She begins to understand something of it all. The joy, that spontaneity of the women on the fields, in fact the cheerfulness of everyone she meets, even the girls who are selling strawberries from wheelbarrows in the street, could it all be ascribed to the fact that the men are gone? They, the men, far away from here in their own isolated world, doing what they enjoy doing most: killing. And the women are free to do what they were born for: nurturing.

The logic is breathtaking. It's always been like this, it's how she herself got to know the world. Now she understands what Aunt Lena meant that time at Bosrand when she said she'd rather see Uncle Thys return in a coffin than surrender before they had their freedom. The men were on commando, and the women controlled the farms. That's how matters stood with her own mother too. Her mother was part of the fierce female chorus that drove the men out and away to those scorched plains. She still remembers how her father was chastised: "Go and fight, we are women enough, your daughter and I, to work with the labourers." To the bitter end it went like that, right to the bitter end! Even after nothing remained of the farmhouses with their porcelain serving dishes and harmoniums, the pantries filled with biltong and preserved peaches and the baking ovens and poultry cages and pigsties and peach orchards and even the occasional kitchen garden, after all of that was destroyed, they remained standing in all their magnificent fury.

When the last chicken was bayonetted and the horses lay rotting in kraals and the plumes of smoke hung over the godforsaken Free State veld and women sat and watched their children coughing away their last breath on a tattered frozen tarpaulin, even then there were those who said with jaws clenched, white as the bone of a stripped sheep carcass: over my dead body. Over my dead body! And there was nothing, no prospects, no hope. Perhaps just the bitterness, the cold blade of bitterness. And she sees them there in that stinking mud hole in the Winburg camp with Uncle Pretorius at the meat table trying to keep the women at bay with a stick, really just a bluebush branch, by swatting at their shins, and the women hissing like angry geese, for her that image of the man with his stick and the furious women are one, you cannot tear them apart, they are inseparable.

"Is something the matter, dear?"

What on earth! Alarmed, Susan looks down, sees how she is gripping her cutlery. Looks up again, and her knife and fork clatter onto the plate as she brings the serviette to her mouth. What's got into her? Things she'd processed years ago were suddenly so present it was as if she could smell and taste and feel them against her skin. She looks directly at Mrs Simms, aware of her anxious expression; she knows she must say something, and when she speaks she does not know where the words come from, or what they have to do with her fear. "But is it necessary for them to gloat like that?" she says, and she knows Mrs Simms has noticed her high colour, she sees her startled gaze.

"Gloat? You mean that they enjoy what they do?" Mrs Simms asked.

"No, no ..." she looks down at her empty plate. "I am sorry, I expressed myself poorly. I just meant that it seems strange to me ..." She forces herself to look at Mrs Simms. "No, not strange, it just struck me that they carry on as if we weren't in a mess, in the middle of an enormous tragedy."

"But what would you have us do?" The older woman drops a serving spoon into a dish and her hands fall to her lap. "Huddle in self-pity with our embroidery and wait for the rescue that may never come? Or do you think everyone should join the Women's Army Auxiliary Corps and go and fight in France? Is that what you think?"

Susan realises that she's made a slip, said the exact opposite of what she meant, in fact. What is it that's upset her so much about the situation, the whole afternoon? It's as if everything that's being said here, everything she experiences, has a direct bearing upon her, that the whole conversation with Mrs Simms is full of insinuations, innuendo, vague allegations. And it's been this way ever since her arrival in England; a lot of old things have been stirred up, she realises, things that have over the years settled like sediment on the seabed of her consciousness, and this woman has stuck her hand in and agitated the dirt. And Susan knows – her training has at least brought that home to her – there is no other option but to throw herself into the turbid waters of her memory. She must go back, in whatever way, to where it all began.

When she replies, she tries to keep her voice even. "I know black people very well. Remember, I come from Africa. Originally."

Mrs Simms frowns: "Oh, ohhh," she says and sits back in her chair, "you're back with the ..."

"Back with the blacks, yes." Susan smiles weakly to reassure the old woman, then quickly continues: "One of the reasons I came here, to work at Seale-Hayne, is because many years ago, when I was still in South Africa, I came across a black man and woman ..." – she wanted to say "knew" but realises that in the context of this conversation it would mean something too intimate, and besides, did she really "know" them? – "I came across black people," she explains, "who in fact led me to psychiatry. It wasn't their intention – on the contrary, they weren't learned people or anything like that – but they just ..." Again she is uncertain what Mrs Simms would be receptive to, or what exactly she wants to say about her experiences in a cave in the war-torn Free State. "The man just told stories," she said. "And the woman ... yes, she was simply very good to me. But one thing I can say is that the man knew how to tell a good story."

Mrs Simms looks even more unsettled, and Susan decides simply to tell one of the stories, the one about the chief who wanted to send his people a message that their suffering would soon end.

Mrs Simms starts clearing the table while Susan speaks, and she realises she is actually telling herself the story, unreal and absurd as it is. It amazes her that she still remembers the details of the story as if she'd heard it yesterday. She hears her own voice at a remove, as if someone else is speaking, as if it's Tiisetso himself talking; his rhythms and intonation become part of her voice, sometimes her tongue wants to imitate the soft Sotho burr; she wants to use these words; she wants to draw the story over her shoulders like a bright blue blanket:

"The chief sent his son to his people with the message. He says to his son: 'Tell my people they will die, but they will rise again.' But the tragedy is that one of the chief's servants heard this and ran to them and said to them, even before the chief's son could get to them, he said to them, and I don't know if it was on purpose or a mistake, he said to them: 'All the people will die and will not rise again.' It is probably no surprise that the name of this false messenger was Gecko. When the chief's son came to bring the real message, when he told them that they would rise again, the people said: 'No, the first message is the first message, what was said was said.' The son persisted, telling them that his father, the chief, had said that they would die and rise again. But the people did not want to hear. 'We don't know you,' they said, 'and Gecko told us that we will not rise again. The first message is the first message. What has been said has been said. And that is how it must be.'"

Susan does not know whether Mrs Simms is still listening. She also does not know how this story could have been healing in any way back then, or what it meant. Back then. But here, in this country and in this war … what does it mean, other than a growing awareness of her own story. Not just the end, but also the beginning.

This is what happened: When she set foot on the slimy, furry concrete of that wharf in Harwich, she had not come from the Netherlands, but directly from her country of birth. She feels the rolling of the mailboat under the thin soles of her shoes; sees again that ghost ship groaning towards them through the mist, and the soldier brushing up against her with his smell of seed and fear. It was all just part of a journey that she began as a young woman, many years ago. She had walked straight from a dusty tarpaulin rising from the desolation of the Free State, a blood-red sun before her, into this country's muted light and fathomless shadows. And when she saw that terraced house in Newton Abbot and heard the English general's name, it was as if nothing had changed, nothing was over.

What has been said has been said. And that is how it must be.

Chapter 14

I could try using my fingertips to drag myself closer to the entrance of the cave. If only I could muster the strength. If only it didn't hurt so much. I must try to get out of here. At some point I have to get out. Where to, I don't know, but what's my life worth, anyway? Perhaps it's for the best to remain in the dark for ever and ever. Perhaps that is the Lord's punishment for me.

Tiisetso sometimes gestures with his knobkerrie when he speaks. He'd stood up suddenly, as if he knew what plans I was making, and so I asked him about the paintings on the ceiling of the cave. He says it's the Baroa who made them, the first people. They are the ones who lived here long ago. They lived here, in these holes, these caves, from the very beginning. They were the very first people on earth. They were the ones who first saw the sun come up. They came out of the holes together with a herd of cattle, and the world was submerged, and above the water weaverbirds hung from the reeds. That is how it was when the first people came out of the cave. The Baroa, they remembered that beginning, and that is what they drew in these caves.

I lie and look at the paintings while Tiisetso sings. He

sings the same words over and over, over and over. In the beginning the words were just sounds to me, altogether incomprehensible, but gradually I began to recognise some of the sounds, like bubbles surfacing in a spring, and plop, making a bright circle in the dark water: *Kea utlwa, mme; kea utlwa, mme ...*

I hear, mother; I hear, I hear. Mother, your voice is like the sparrow, the weaver; your voice is like the weaver hanging from the reed.

He stops singing, but continues to rock backwards and forwards. Then he speaks. Look, he says, and points at the paintings against the cave wall. You must go and fetch your own cattle, like those people, the Baroa. You must go and fetch them, far, far, far, far. You must walk that road. Far, all the way to the *badimo*. But you must walk that road, you must walk that road. The speckled cow, the one with spots like a guinea fowl, the colourful one, that is the cow.

I know what Tiisetso means. I am not stupid. As if I have time for their ancestor-worshipping nonsense. I believe in God. He will help me. Tiisetso can talk and sing all he wants, for all I care. If I pray, my thoughts will reach heaven; I must just find the right words. And I must pray that the Lord takes this terrible thing from me, because it's a great, great sin. I don't know if Tiisetso is saying that it's I who brought the sin upon the land, and that he and Mamello are fattening me up for sacrifice so that the sins of the country may be forgiven. But I am not the only one, hear me, Lord, I am not the only one. What about the English burning down farms and letting everyone die in the camps? Is that not also a sin in the eyes of the Lord? I will pay for my sins, but the Lord does not sleep. He will also make the English pay.

I don't mind if Tiisetso sings, at least then I know someone is here with me. I don't mind, he can sing all he wants. I know the song by now, the one about the weaverbird hanging from the reed.

I know the tune and the words by now and I can already sing along with him. And I've noticed that if I do, if I keep singing, then it's as if I become light and start floating. It takes me away from the things that claw into my thoughts.

It's probably people like Oupa and Ouma that Tiisetso is talking about. People who died long ago. It's probably their voices that cling like weaverbirds to the reeds that shiver in the mud. I hear you, Ma, I hear, I hear … I hear you, Pa, I hear, I hear. In fact, I haven't been able to hear Pa's voice for a long time, his voice was already lost to me in the camp. Now he stands like a reed and shakes in that mud from which the first people emerged like a herd of cattle from a kraal. He is in my head now. Pa. Like cattle walking in the long grass, Pa came into my head, like that speckled cow, or like a horse galloping alongside a fence with its head held high. That is Pa.

Pa had fetched his stallion from the kraal, while Ma and I stood on either side of the horse. The horse kicked at flies, and I'd giggled. Because I did not know what else to do. All I can remember is the horse farting as it trotted across the yard, each step a pff-pff-pff.

The next thing we heard, Pa was dead. Right at the beginning of the war. Many of the men in the district hadn't even gone on commando yet.

Heilbron's own field cornet had brought the news; he hadn't left yet either. Ma sat up straight in the sitting room. Neels's mouth hung slack. Uncle Hennie and Aunt Lena had come with the field cornet, and they all just stood there. The field cornet asked whether the children could go out and play. I let my head drop and Ma said I was no longer a child and the field cornet should say what he had come to say.

I watched Neels and saw how a long shiny strip of spittle hung from his bottom lip. When I picked him up to take him outside he clung to Ma's chair. I almost had to break his hands open. I still remember it. How much strength I had to use to bend open his little-boy fingers and how he started moaning. Like a small animal or something.

A month later it was just me and Ma and Neels in the share-cropper's cottage. Aunt Lena stayed behind in the big house. And the workers too. It was only us on the farm. All the men were gone. Most of Pa's horses also, gone with the men on commando. All that remained was the piebald mare Pa had broken in for me before he left. The first time Pa mounted her she jumped and jumped until she fell. Pa kept clinging on.

She gave a sigh as she fell, it looked as if she was winded, because her mouth was open and her tongue curled back as she tried to breathe. After that you could ride her, but she was as stubborn as a mule. Tsela rode her, but he only managed to get her into a short gallop once or twice. He brought the cattle to the house sometimes so that I could help with the counting. Then the piebald mare would stand dead still at the kraal gate and it always seemed to me that she was looking at me with Pa's eyes.

That mare only foaled once. A stallion had jumped the fence. Pa locked her up in the kraal for a while, and then the stallion came neighing around the kraal and kicked his forelegs up against the gate ... and ... and ... I saw it all, it's too terrible, dear Lord Jesus, what is to become of me, because I couldn't kick and bite like that mare, and although there was a gate and a kraal the mare's stomach swelled until she went and lay in the grass and from the house I could see how she lifted her head and bent her neck backwards to see what was happening. Afterwards I went and had a look and saw there was a wet spot with blood close by and dung and hoofmarks dug into the ground.

I hadn't even noticed that Tiisetso had stopped singing. Dear God, Tiisetso, please! Why did you stop? Sing, for God's sake, just sing! You can't stop, not now, please! You can't stop now, please, not now! You must sing for me so that my thoughts can flow, like cattle leaving a kraal, so that I can take the footpaths that my feet know so well, the warm sand soft under my bare feet.

The veld is bare, there's barely a blade of grass left, just Pa's body with the soft velvet of his jacket collar, the one Ma turned, and the cloud of bluebottles that you can see from afar, that is where Pa is lying. Come look, Ma says, and bring Neels. We follow the cloud. Like blue coals those bluebottle bodies glow in the night, and we sit and watch afterwards as if by a fire. Listening to the buzzing that grows louder and louder until everything, everything is just buzzing bluebottles.

Chapter 15

She wakes up, startled. A staff member is leaning over her; light falls through the open door into the nurses' station. In the half-light Susan recognises the face above her. There is a new arrival, the nurse says, and a senior nurse should be present while he is admitted.

Susan rinses her face at the washstand – she'd come to lie down on the narrow hospital bed long after midnight, and fallen asleep in her clothes. A few hours of uninterrupted sleep is a luxury when you do night shift here, because for most of the patients the night is also the darkest time of the day.

Uncomplainingly she accompanies the nurse to the courtyard – she would have had to get up in a few minutes' time anyway to help with the morning routines. There are soldiers who must be woken and helped with the morning toilet and with dressing, and then readied for breakfast where every mouthful has to be carefully monitored. She asks if help is needed; sometimes severely disturbed patients need to be drugged. But the girl shakes her head.

The olive-green army vehicle stands parked inside the courtyard as usual when patients are brought in. There seems to be only one patient, and he just stands there, like a dark pole sticking out of white gravel in the dawn. It is rare to receive a single patient; usually there's a group, accompanied by a swarm of orderlies and nurses, either being supported, constrained or sometimes even carried.

He turns silently towards her when she is close by. Pale, lips sealed, infinitely tired, it seems. He has an officer's rank, she sees, and the driver stands expectantly next to them with his military bag.

"Shall I show you?" Susan asks. The lieutenant nods, and she leads the small procession to the reception hall where the initial evaluation will take place, with an immediate decision on the treatment to be followed. She makes him sit on one of the four beds; the orderly puts the bag down and excuses himself. Susan fetches a clipboard with forms and a pen and sits on a chair next to the bed. As with most newcomers, he does not look at her. Most of them don't say a word, answer curtly and absent-mindedly when questioned, or sometimes not at all. He, however, speaks in full, if muted, sentences, and with a weary sigh in his voice: name, rank, unit, combat zone ... the basic details. She ensures that her voice is soft, sympathetic — that is the first principle of medical care in this hospital. Patients must be assisted in taking hold of a thread of humanity, a thread they themselves must unravel until there's something soft for them again beside the vicious barbed wire of the war.

"Do you know why you were sent here?" she asks.

He nods.

"One of the doctors will do the medical check-up later on, but could you perhaps try to describe your symptoms to me?"

100

He wipes his face and his eyes leap at her and then away again, as if terrified. "Sleep," he says. "I simply cannot fall asleep. And if sleep does eventually come, I dream. About the war." He has an anxious look on his face and it seems that he needs to concentrate hard on what he is saying, or make an effort to remember what it is he wants to say. "The light has to stay on all the time otherwise I can't sleep, in the dark every little noise makes me jolt upright. I no longer want to go to bed because …" He looks down at his legs, his hands pressed flat on either side of him, "because I simply cannot get the thoughts out of my head."

"Do you have any references, medical reports?"

He sticks his hand inside his coat and takes a notebook from a pocket, opens it on his lap, and gives her the folded form that's been pressed between the pages. She reads as he pages through the notebook, trying perhaps to keep his hands busy.

The certificate describes a wound he received in France. An explosion had buried him under a pile of soil, and while he was busy excavating himself a bullet hit him in the arm. He was sent home, to a London hospital. There were notes about nervous symptoms, insomnia, and loss of appetite.

"Did you go back again after London?" she asks.

He speaks in a dejected tone, his fingers fiddling with the notebook. "After the wound healed I went to a rehabilitation place in the countryside," he says. "Northumberland." He looks up at her, then shifts his gaze away from her face, to something just to the left of her. "But the dreams kept coming. Hardly ever slept and became more fearful by the day that I would never recover."

"But you haven't come from the rehabilitation centre; according to your report, you've come down from London?"

"I thought the only way to get better was to return to my battalion, but the medical board had to approve it. When I appeared in front of the board I told them I was fine, but then they asked after my sleeping patterns. There was something about that in the report from the centre. Then they sent me here."

"Do you know what to expect here?" she asks.

He shrugs. "I know that it's a mental home, that's all."

"This is a hospital," she says. "We treat war wounds. You have a medical condition, a wound to the spirit, and it can be treated."

He stares at her, and for the first time he looks her straight in the eye. "You're not English," he says.

She returns his gaze, for a moment they size each other up. "You're right," she says coolly. "I am not. I am Dutch."

He looks away. She looks down at the clipboard on her lap, considers making an entry, but doesn't really know what to write. "You'll have to wait here a while," she then says. "The doctor should be here in an hour or so. But it's quiet enough, maybe you'll get some rest." She gets up and looks down at his bowed forehead. "The staff nurse will come and sit with you. Mere routine. You can ask her if you need anything."

She walks down the hallway with the clipboard pressed against her chest. There is no one else about; the hospital will become busy only in an hour or so. What was it that happened there a moment ago? Why do these things affect me so personally? It's as if I'm a novice, a child, as if my emotions were a ball of mercury in a teaspoon.

She leans with her back against the wall, her chin on her chest. She can't get rid of the feeling that something in this situation, however strange and new it might be, is also very familiar to her. Something constantly threatening to reveal itself. Even in this conversation with the officer. Oh, well, she doesn't really know what it is, perhaps his vulnerability? But also the patronising way in which he asked about her nationality. It was confrontational, aggressive, as if he had to defend himself, as if he were in the trenches again, and she, the one meant to help him, was his assailant. Yes, there was something dangerous in the situation; it was a war by proxy, there in the reception hall. Or is that just her perception? He is, after all, utterly at the mercy of this thing, not her, but this war that has ripped his soul out. And that's why she's come here, for the sake of people like him. From the very beginning the mere thought of it was ... yes, what exactly? Exciting? Daring? The kind of thing she needs as much as she needs oxygen?

Now she knows. Now she knows. That's what Jacques felt back then, that everything for her was a gamble. It has something to do with risk, that she now knows for sure. That's why those rides on Jacques's motorbike were such a relief for her, because she felt the urge, and he was available. She had to risk shrieking wildly while being hurled through the streets of Dordrecht on the back of his bike, or hanging onto his arm and pushing open the doors of a bar. Yes, that's what frightened him. He could see her lust for life, her fearlessness.

She shudders, pushing away from the wall with the back

of her head and starts walking, unseeing, with a slight sway. She had to risk taking hold of his pale fingertips and pushing them against the softness, the tautness of her bodice. And Jacques was mute with terror. He was frightened of who and what she was.

Hurst grants her an hour a day to give music therapy to a hand-picked group of patients. He helped her with the selection, convinced of its value, though they weren't in full agreement about its focus. She was enthusiastic about the hospital's programmes to occupy patients with various tasks. "Yes, draw their attention away from their morbid self-absorption," she'd said.

Hurst looked at her sternly and said: "Not everyone is self-absorbed."

When he said that, she knew she'd used the wrong word. "I mean …" Immediately realising it was a rather desperate effort, she persevered nonetheless. "I mean that they're so focused on this darkness within that one should try to draw their attention away from it."

"That won't take the darkness away," he said, and she had the sense of something dark in his voice too.

She kept quiet, waiting for him to lead the conversation to its logical conclusion, as she knew she'd spoken against her better judgement, completely at odds with her own belief – the necessity of confronting the darkness within oneself.

The corner of his mouth twitched, as if he'd briefly considered a cordial smile. He starts speaking in a measured way, circumspect, his sentence a wave that builds up slowly then breaks away foaming as it washes out far into the distance. "What I do think you can achieve with the music is to fill their negative experiences with a new energy, a new light, give a new colour to it, something positive to connect it with. Perhaps they'd come into contact again with the camaraderie they'd known, the companionship. It might not seem so now, but there is something positive out there, there is." He lifted a finger to an eyebrow and the shadow of his hand fell over his face; she had listened to him silently and nodded attentively.

In the music room the heavy velvet curtains are drawn and the light on its slim copper stand is on, but the room remains dim. It's as if the men gathering around the piano had elbowed out the light, as if their bodies absorbed all the available glow. They sing with gaping mouths and staring eyes: "It's the soldiers of the King, my lads, who've been, my lads, who've seen, my lads …" The voices fill the room, press up against the roof, the pianist reclines on his chair, throwing his head back as if trying to balance a sailboat.

Susan stands at the piano stool, conducting with one hand, maintaining eye contact to ensure momentum, so that they keeping singing lustily, creating a chain of song between the darkness and the light.

Out of the corner of her eye she sees a movement at the door. Hurst. He listens for a while, seemingly preoccupied, then lifts a long, pale finger to his temple.

And with that momentary distraction, during that break in the unceasing vigilance she expects of herself, those old images slip in. She blinks her eyes, smiles in surprise – now where does that come from? The burghers, threadbare warriors with sunken cheeks standing in an open railway truck singing "Praise the Lord" en route to damnation, and in a bone-white bell tent the women sing "*Naar de oorlog moest ik gaan; voor de kogels moest ik staan*", the bagpipes, flutes and drums with "God Save the King", and Tiisetso and Mamello singing and singing and singing about birds that fly low over the earth, over a herd of cattle walking along a vlei. She turns her head to Hurst, she knows his eyes are shaded, she knows he is looking at her standing among the men, caught up in the sound bubble of their voices, swaying on the breeze of the piano's melody.

This is where I must stay, she thinks, woven into this experience, inside this bubble, this is my calling. But she slips away, battling to concentrate, like doves fluttering up from a bluegum her thoughts break away from her and fly up against the sun of another continent. She forces them back, back to where she is now, to where she is supposed to be, but then she is bumping around on the back seat of a motorcar, with Hurst in the passenger seat, and Jacobs at the wheel. They are going to Dartmoor, it is the hospital's day on the shooting range. Here at the hospital the patients are singing and she is conducting, but her thoughts are on the bumpy ride through Dartmoor's russet and green fields, between the hillocks and rocky peaks known as "tors". They are en route to the military rifle range where Hurst permits some of the patients to recreate the battlefields of Flanders in order to reconnect them with what had previously kept them going.

She stands with the wind against her back; Jacobs leans

against the motorcar's mudguard and he squeezes his words through his teeth, dropping them onto the heather, onto the wet turf that sucks at their shoes. Some of the words remain hanging in the air; she peers into the wind and Jacobs's voice presses in from behind, her nurse's uniform flapping around her legs. Before her, a bewildered platoon comes marching towards Hurst, who is waiting at a trench-and-bunker construction. The soldiers run towards the barbed-wire obstacles and breastwork, knock in more stakes, double sentries are set out, including one for a gas attack – Lewis-snipers who will have to kneel in the dark. From inside the bunker, soldiers dig away at shooting slits to extend their arc of fire, streams of grey rain, the water in the trench gushes like … like the Laaispruit in flood, she thinks, the barbed wire along the railway track through the Karoo, wooden crosses where soldiers had died, a train pulling farther and farther away from where she had lain. She balls her fists next to her sides, she straightens her back like a shield against Jacobs's voice that comes at her from behind, like the wind blowing and blowing, relentlessly.

As the platoon of patients comes marching past, Jacobs begins his tale – the story of the patient in front on the left, the short one, the one lifting his knees right up to his ears, like a madman. "Do you see him," Jacobs says, and his voice flies like shrapnel, "… and the explosion threw him five, six feet into the air, he landed on his head, onto a man lying there, fell right into the swollen belly of a German who'd been dead a few days already …" She shuffles her feet and the sods sucking at her soles make a smacking noise. "And when he hit the rotten corpse, everything burst open. Yes, he passed out then, but before he passed out, he – ugh, Jesus! – he felt his mouth full of something and he tasted – fuck – sorry about saying this, but you'll understand, sorry – he knew it was the rotten innards of an enemy, he knew it. When he came to, he puked and puked for days on end, but he couldn't get rid of it, that taste and that smell, and that's why he was sent to us. That's his story. Sorry, I know you're a woman and all, but, yes, that's how it was."

She sees Hurst walking towards them and she runs to meet him, lifting her dress and almost stumbling in her haste. "Is it a good thing?" she asks when she sees his eyes in their dark sockets. "Is it? This return to …" She can't find the word. "Is it necessarily a good thing to … to go back to that which almost destroyed you?"

Hurst gives a quick step forward, his arms outstretched to prevent her from falling. He talks as they walk, into the wind, shouting: "Only if the patient can supplement his experiences with a new energy, tap some positive energy out of it again," he says, and comes to a halt. She feels as if he's trained a pair of binoculars on her, watching and analysing her every movement. "There are some of them that pick up a gun, ready to shoot again," he says, and looks away from her, making a wide, helpless gesture with his hand. "Ready for the slaughter."

Ready for the slaughter. Slaughter? Her thoughts reach out tentatively at the word. It was hardly the first time she'd returned to her past; she has after all been schooled in psychiatry and one of the core principles is to know yourself, your potential and your shortcomings, where you come from and where you are going, but there on that marsh with its woolly vegetation, its shallow waterways, its tufts of cloud, there she tried for the first time to make the word "slaughter" her own. And yet, and yet ... was it not her word all along? Literally. The ewe that is pulled by her kicking hind leg into the tent: I have been there who knows how many times. I have found all the necessary words to talk about it, but is it good, is it healing to return to that tent? I don't know. I don't know.

She blinks once or twice then sees the singing, swaying heads in front of her again. "It's the soldiers of the King, my lads, who've been, my lads, who've seen, my lads ..." To the right of her the door is now closed. Hurst has left. She raises both hands. She stands woman alone against the onslaught of nothing less than history itself: A young woman wearing a bonnet is playing a harmonium that has just been carried from the house, she plays against the barking of the first flames, she plays "Rots der eeuwen", her bonnet drooping over the keys, and around her, scattered across the bare yard, are many other women who are laughing crazily, lurching about singing hysterically, bent double, their arms dangling, and then running into the veld completely out of their mind. And here at the hospital in Devon she raises her hands passionately – no, wildly – before the beaming, clean-shaven faces and gaping mouths, she holds her hands up in the surging sound, and she sees them all in this twilight room with the piano and the lamp and the curtains, everything part of a continuous stream that has flowed unstoppably since the very beginning through everything, dragging along both the living and the dead, and in that vast torrent of time she is standing in a prehistoric cave and holding her hands up high; she presses her hands against a rock wall that is crawling with little people, hunters with bloody noses and ecstatic erections descending into the darkness where the great big light lies hidden, down down down towards the dark light.

Eventually she drops her hands, heavy as lead and throbbing painfully, and simply sings, she sings uncomplainingly as if illuminated by that first light, singing along to songs that for someone must bring back something of value.

Chapter 16

When Mamello speaks, one may as well listen. What else. At least they bring me food, she and old Tiisetso. Sometimes there's a pot on my fire, boiling away, and sometimes they carry it in to me. From where, I have no idea. Green stuff as well. *Marôgo*. Tender cooked meat. Pap. Plenty of curdled milk. *Marôgo* with slimy rabbit meat in a dish, and then she places the pot of pap next to it, pushing the *lesokana* down through the cloud of steam so as to stir the pap again. They're looking after me.

In the beginning she fed me, but now I feed myself. Scooping the porridge up with my hand and then making a little ball. Dipping it into the sauce. Sometimes when the green taste of the plants and the brown taste of the meat together with the warm white steam of the mealie meal fills my mouth it is as if I have been waiting for this for ever, for my whole life. All the time in the camp that we spent waiting for food, praying for it, fighting for it in the queues. It was for this, for what I have now. In the camp we sometimes did things just to forget about food, like sitting and singing in one of the tents or playing kennetjie in the dust outside. Or we did this so that we wouldn't think about dying.

The food also keeps things out of my head. While I'm chewing, when there's something in my mouth, that feeling of just wanting to die goes away a bit. And when I've eaten, it's also easier to do some of the things that they want me to do.

She is slightly shorter than me, Mamello. I can see it when she helps me up. Also, the hairs around her thin neck are already grey. Her collar is rather loose, and there's a blackish ointment on the inside of it. But it's me who stinks so, I realise that now, it's me. Dirty, rotten sinfulness.

It's a struggle down the incline and over the loose stones in front of the cave. First we have to get through the thick koeniebos, but Mamello helps me with the bending and crawling. It was she who told me to come, and not for the usual reason. We've already gone farther than the distance I go every day to attend to my private needs. I usually just go to the left, between a clump of kwarriebossies.

Down in the undergrowth, in the ravines that run between the ridges, there must be a stream and that is where she is taking me, I assume. She won't be able to take me all the way to Laaispruit, because I'd noticed whenever I went with the camp children to fetch wood there that the low hills where I'm now living are much farther away. When I asked whether someone might not see us, she said Tiisetso is watching, he is sitting up there, he'll be on the lookout.

She's in fact just brought me to a rocky ridge in the bushes. With a hole here and there that seems to have filled up after yesterday's – no, when? – rain. She kneels easily for an old person, this Mamello. She seems able to do so more easily than I can, just folding her legs in under her dress and sitting down.

112

Yes, let her remove the rags from my head, because the things that were between my legs have already been thrown away.

It's a long strip that she has to unwind, I notice, and bits of it look like compacted dung. Disgusting!

But it doesn't hurt. It no longer hurts at all.

She takes a cake of soap from her pocket and puts it on the rock and takes hold of my dress below my arms – and yes, let me get up so that she can pull the dress over my shoulders. But stand in front of her I will not, not completely naked like this. If only the sun hadn't made the stone so hot to the touch and the pebbles didn't poke at my bottom in this way. But it feels good, the sun on my back, the cool breeze on my shoulder blades. Look at the gooseflesh here on my forearms. Here on my ribs. And the bruises, one would swear I was a guinea fowl.

Mamello kneels next to the water and washes her hands and arms. When they're wet like this, they shine like pebbles and her palms are as white as bone. My arms look purple with hairs standing on end.

I don't know if that dress of mine has ever been so dirty. But it's the only clothing I have. Mamello has washed it once or twice, and then I sit naked for a while under the blanket. That stain on the dress. She'll see it, the old girl. She's probably seen it already. When it happened in the camp I always washed my clothes myself. And at home the first time, I didn't yet know that the blood would come monthly. In the camp Ma had rags stitched for me by one of the aunties who had a machine in her tent.

Luckily Mamello is holding my hand, because the stone bed of this pool is pretty slippery. And the water is cold. My toes ache from the cold.

And does she have to splash the water against my legs, and so high! I might even swallow my tongue.

She begins to soap me, and her headscarf is around my knees, the soap smooth on my skin. With one hand around my left knee she pulls my legs open.

Here, I say, she must give me the soap, I'm old enough, at least. I can do it myself from here.

Even though I'm standing with my back to her, I can feel how she is looking at me. Her eyes and the sun on my back. Dirty suds run down my thighs. How many days' dirt? Now I see more bruises. I can't press too hard. Just my upper body and face, quickly, then I'll be finished, even though I rather like the clouds of soapy water in the pool.

I know only too well by now what *tlo ke tla o thusa* means – come let me help you. I put the soap in Mamello's hand, and before I can stop her she bends down in front of me, one hand in the hollow of my back while with the other she begins to soap between my legs, that hand like a little animal in and out of my groin. Wait! I grab her wrist, and she looks up at me, don't, for heaven's sake! But a sob snatches my words away. I cry and I cry. It's the first time since I've been in the cave, I think, the first time that I've cried.

Mamello looks up at me, her eyes as milky as the soapy water. A droplet falls from me onto her face and she blinks. My child, she says, my child, and I allow her to carry on washing me, gently, gently.

Sometimes when you sit in the sun like this it's as if your thoughts slow down until they come to a standstill.

Mamello and I must wait for my dress to dry. She left so that I could continue washing myself, there in the pool. I washed and washed, and then Mamello also washed my dress in the pool. The two of us scrubbed; she scrubbed until that stain was gone, but I was not finished yet. I don't know, but it felt to me as if I would never be clean again.

Mamello spread the dress over one of the rocks and then went and stood in one of the pools and began stomping up and down in the mud. As she stepped she clapped her hands and sang: *Pête, pête tlo nku ke, mme ha n rate, ke ratwa ke lefatse lena ...* And every now and then she looked at me, the dear old girl, and she said I must come and join her. It was still quite sore to walk, not to mention dance, but I did. *Pête, pête,* we stamped our feet in the mud that splattered higher and higher up our legs, and I forgot about my stiff legs and danced completely naked with her, I clapped and I sang *pête, pête,* and our voices went higher and higher, come and take me, my mother does not love me, this soil loves me, *pête, pête ...* And strangely I felt much cleaner like this, smeared in mud. Now we are sitting on the warm rock and my heart is beating faster from the mud song. Mamello sits apart with my dress between us on the ledge.

At first I sat bunched up with my knees held against my body, but now I am sitting like her, with my legs out in front of me. And my thoughts are slow and lazy, and Mamello is still singing softly. Occasionally a sob heaves up in me, like it does when one has been crying. I try to remember why

I was crying, and I know it is because something very bad happened to me.

And I also know what happened, but I'm getting better now and that's what is most important, that I become completely healthy again. And I know why Mamello sang the song and danced and took me with in her song. I know why. In the blood she saw that the thing did not come and lie in my stomach. With her song she spoke to me and also with the God of heaven and earth who arranged that I would be placed in the hands of these people and in that cave.

When Mamello and I reach the cave again, Tiisetso is waiting. I scrunch up my dress in front of me in case something shows through, but he doesn't even look. He has something folded in his hands, holds it out to me, and I must take it carefully, hold it so that it doesn't fall.

It's some living thing and I get such a fright that I almost drop the little creature, but luckily Tiisetso keeps holding on too. He probably knew that I'd get a fright.

It's a little meerkat. He is warm and prickly in my hands, his little nails are quite sharp, but I feel his little heart beating, his small wet snout nosing through my fingers.

Now I have to lie down, because I'm feeling weak. The little creature comes to lie with me under the blanket, and I will hold him softly. Softly.

Let Tiisetso and Mamello stand there and look at me as if they were my mother and father. They are not. I will get better, and then when the war is over, I will look up everyone who was with me in tent 19. Perhaps I could, like Chrissie Barnard and Maggie Pelser, become a nurse.

Anyway, I imagine that the little meerkat will be big by the time the burghers return, by the time they return to raise the flag of the Republic again.

I lie for ages just feeling the little meerkat's heartbeat and how he sometimes wiggles his nose. And there where I lie it suddenly dawns on me: I'd clean forgotten to look for a way to escape this cave.

Chapter 17

Hurst pushes the patient's folder over the table towards her with his fingertips. His nails are clipped short, she sees, too short. "It looks good, your music programme," he says.

"Is this someone you want me to take on?" she asks without looking at him, barely seeing the name on the folder, instinctively shutting her eyes, like the moment just before a bug flies into your face, or just before ... yes, just before a whiskey bottle hits you. She keeps her eyes shut, her head down, trying to hook her thoughts onto something else. Too short, she thinks, his nails have been cut too short, and she opens her eyes and fixes her gaze on Hurst's face.

"Not necessarily," he says, "but I would like to know what you think. It's a serious case, and I haven't been able to achieve much so far. The door remains shut to me."

"What have you tried? Hypnosis?"

"Hypnosis. Hypnotic medication. What do you use in the Netherlands, also Medinal? When he was admitted, he suffered from serious insomnia. At that stage he was still speaking. Just said that he couldn't sleep. No details. Just that: I can't sleep. I explained to him that the solution doesn't lie in getting away from the memories, and that it probably wouldn't help to try to forget. You know the story: that we should rather find ways to make his memories more bearable."

"Do you think ..." Then she forgets what she wants to say; she inhales deeply, keeping her eyes on Hurst.

He hesitates briefly and then continues: "Look, I've often found that people don't respond positively immediately, but with him it was as if the mere mention – the possibility of recovery – would upset him. I said what I normally say, namely that, instead of these demonic forces that overwhelm him at night, we should try to make pleasant companions of the things that cause him so much suffering. His eyes immediately rolled over and he started shaking. Refused to speak. Aspirin and bromide helped him sleep a bit better, but even with massage it's as if his whole body becomes an impenetrable shell, becoming harder and harder. I thought I'd try once more before I ... well, would have to report that he's of no more use to the army."

She watched Hurst as he spoke: his clean, almost transparent face, his thin mouth and sunken eyes, fingertips at times hooking on to the edge of the table. "Do you think he's reacting against you?" she then said – she had a hunch. "I don't mean your personality of course, that goes without saying. It's just that you're the embodiment of ..." Then it occurs to her that his severely clipped nails might be a contradiction of what she is saying, yet she perseveres: "An embodiment of wholeness." Perhaps he chews his nails down. It could be nerves, and he is not as whole and as self-contained as he seems.

His gaze remains fixed on her, which unnerves her even more. An irritability stirs in her; she pushes her back against the chair.

He is not the one who is irritating her, she thinks, not exactly, it's rather ... what? My own touchiness? She has to think for a moment to get back on track, and when she starts speaking she is aware of the fact that her voice is pitched too high: "I'm just thinking of something that Dr Rivers once said, that he believed his success could partly be ascribed to the fact that he too bore some kind of wound. His speech impediment perhaps, I don't know, perhaps his patients also sensed something else. A sense of inferiority?"

Before she said the last word she started doubting herself, and her statement became a question. She looks into Hurst's eyes – not for understanding, but for a sign that he might be offended. Understanding and sympathy are the last thing she wants now, she'd rather give offence. "Sorry, I'm casting about in the dark a bit here."

He keeps watching her, and now there is a slight frown between his eyes: "I doubt Rivers said this himself," he says, lost in thought. "It was perhaps said about him ..."

"But it's true, isn't it? Is it unprofessional of me to say so? I am sorry if it is, I just ..."

He waves her excuses away impatiently. "I don't know if it is true," he says hoarsely. "He is a colleague and I don't want to ..." he falls silent, looks at her questioningly for a moment, the frown now deeper. "Do you think that's why I asked you?"

"Why?"

"Do you think I asked you because I think you have some flaw that he could identify with?"

She hadn't seen that one coming. Is Hurst making her

pay for her disrespect? Is that how men support each other? "What flaw might this be?" She hears the chill in her voice. "Because I am a woman?"

He repeats the dismissive hand gesture. "That is not a weakness, surely?" He does not, however, give her the opportunity to answer. "Forget it," he says, pressing both hands down on the desk, leaning forward so that his chest almost touches the edge of it, as if he wants to physically steer the conversation in another direction, wants to leap onto it like a tiger. "I understand you in fact come from South Africa," he says slowly, pulling himself up in his chair.

She feels the adrenaline prickling in her fingertips, tries to answer, but only manages a hoarse cough. How does he know! Did he hear it from Anne?

"Experienced something of that war, perhaps?" In his own way he is careful, but still feline.

She coughs, trying to get her voice under control. "Do you think that is a weakness? That I come from South Africa?"

He does not answer her, and she realises he does not have to. She is being completely preposterous, touchy. She is actually showing him a wound, and he is clever enough to notice. "Rivers," she then says – she must get away from here – "he made much of the traditional medicines of primitive people."

He nods slowly, lost in thought, clearly watching her footwork very attentively. "That's not why I brought it up, but yes, you're right. What is it that you had in mind?"

"That's one thing that I gained in South Africa," she says hesitantly, faltering, not sure what direction she is taking with this, perhaps just a headlong dash to get away.

121

"I think that's what made me come here, the fact that I too have a certain admiration for such traditional practices, you could probably call it a form of belief." She falls silent, lowering her eyes before his searching gaze. Meerkat eyes, she suddenly thinks, and looks up, but he speaks before she can examine this impression that's come to mind.

"Belief," he says, "yes, that does play a role. In this case, though, it's not a question of my belief – I firmly believe in my approach – but rather that of the patient. He no longer believes in any possibilities. I don't think he wants to believe any more."

That patient, they can talk about that later, but first she has to … she must first … "Yes, I was in that war," she then says. Is that what he wants to know? Is that what this is all about? Then it has to be said, and the sooner the better.

He nods, his eyes somewhere in their dark sockets. "Take a look at that folder," he says.

"Do you want me to include him in the music programme?" she asks again, and keeps looking at him.

"I just want to know what you think," he says. "Perhaps you have a solution?"

"But you do think that it has something to do with the fact that I come from South Africa?"

"It's a vague theory," he says. "Perhaps I am grasping at straws."

She looks down, this time directly at the folder on her lap, reading the inked letters, without taking anything in at first, but a hazy suspicion sharpens into focus, an old suspicion, at first vague and then ominous and close, and suddenly there, like lightning in the room: the name, the one that was there the minute Hurst pushed the file across to her, that name was there and that is what dragged her down so treacherously into this quicksand of things that cannot be said. She blinks repeatedly, and only then can she look up and speak more or less evenly: "And you want me to ... involve ... him?"

He shrugs, looks at her silently for a while, and then quickly stands up. "Come," he says, "it's perhaps better if you see for yourself."

She drops the file on the desk and gets up, two short strides and she is with Hurst, behind him, not wanting to be far away from him now, not in this dark haunted house. She is a child, a child. And she walks next to him, almost up against him, and she barely looks down the hallway, but keeps her eyes on him, on his calm, clean, reasonable male head.

And now they stand in front of the door. In front of a dark unyielding surface, its edge against the doorframe. She stands in front of that reflecting surface, the tiny varnish cracks like the retina of an eye, the smell of polished wood in her nostrils, her breath against the unforgiving surface, and she knows, she knows there is a name on the white label in the small metal holder, and it is a name that she cannot utter.

She turns around to Hurst, who has remained standing behind her. Her face averted so that he will not notice her shock, her fingertips behind her against the wood. Hurst is speaking, but she does not hear him. With one hand he gently pushes her aside, and with the other he opens the door. She follows him into the gloom, the back of his smoothly ironed uniform between her and the bed, between her and the man in the bed. Slowly, she shuffles closer. He is lying with his back to her; his head is turned towards drab curtains that hang dead still at the window. From behind, she sees only a profile: the ear a dark fold on the equally dark hunk of his head. If there was light, she thought, his ear would be transparent, rosy and fine-veined against the glare, perhaps peeling a little along the rim of its wing-like curve. This is what she has been trained to do, to see light and life. That is her purpose here. But in the gloom everything is upended. Or perhaps exactly as it should be: the ear a handle to grip the head and pull it sideways so that the eyes look up at you and you look down into the depths of the pupils to look for ... the Lord alone knows, to look for recognition, because this ear has a mark, the lobe is gone, and it is her mark.

It is her mark.

Her tongue sticks to her palate, loosens with a smacking sound. There is something inside her, like a whirlwind ripping sticks and dust from the dry veld and hurling them into the searing blue skies. She cannot stop it. It is there: her teeth biting through cartilage until tooth grinds against tooth. She wants to taste something; she wants to fill her mouth with it. She wants the warm metallic taste, she wants to feel a lump of flesh in her mouth, she wants to push it with the tip of her tongue through her teeth, wants to spit it out, vomit it out. With her fingertips she pushes her ears closed, drops her chin to her chest, shuts her eyes tight tight tight to stop it, to keep it at bay.

How long had she been standing there? She does not know, aware only of a swishing silence. Where does it come from?

What has happened to me? This is not what I came here for. It was never there before. Not like this.

She slowly drops her hands to her side. The reeling has abated. No, it was never like that, she now realises. I was never granted that sensation. I never tasted that satisfaction. He did scream, that I do remember. Oh yes, he yelped like a goddamned dog. He grabbed the bottle that was standing on the table next to the bed, and then came the shattering blow against my head.

That is all.

She looks at the door that has clicked shut behind them. The door with his name on it. Something – somebody? – whips her around so that she stands with her back to the bed. She only realises that she has been holding her breath once she lets it out in gasps. How did I land up here? she wonders. Why am I here in this ordinary, quiet, clinical, lightless room? Is that not what I'd asked for? I wanted … God, yes, what did I want? To hear a fighter plane sputter through shredded clouds, I wanted to see cannons rearing up in the mud, I wanted to see a sky filled with shrapnel and flames, and a firmament filled with lamentation. I want a war, not the silence of this dim room with its sheets that are like a doily on a jug of sour milk!

But it remains deathly silent in the room. Just the silence. Eventually, Hurst's body does begin to stir under the fabric of his uniform, and his voice, coming from somewhere, from where Hurst's mouth should be, there, near the bed – from there it comes, as if the man himself is speaking. Speaking to her. "Colonel Henry Hamilton-Peake," says the voice.

That name that she cannot say. And she sees him coming. He comes marching down the road between the tents, the sun aslant on his shoulders, dust on his boots. She and her friend Alice come dawdling from the opposite end, and Alice gently pushes her out of the way. "Look," Alice says, "there he comes, Hamilton." She blows her cheeks out, as if her mouth were stuffed with porridge. "Hamilton-Peake," Alice says.

"What?" she answers wide-eyed, clowning around. "Hamilton-Puke?"

They fall about laughing among the tents. Alice hanging onto her, he looking back angrily, she pulling her dress back over her shoulder, the sun like shimmering spears between the white bell tents, Alice's laugh turning into a coughing fit.

"Sister Nell?"

What? It's Hurst talking. Here, next to her. She sees feet making a peak under a sheet. She tries to focus. The sheet twitches.

This is where she is, with Dr Arthur Hurst at the Seale-Hayne Hospital in Devon. Not in Winburg's concentration camp. And yet nothing has changed. Nothing is over. Nothing is ever completely over.

He guides her out of the door and softly pulls it shut behind them. Her eyes narrow in the harsh light. She notices that Hurst is looking at her with concern, but then straightaway he starts to stride ahead. "Everything okay?" he asks once they're in step.

She nods.

"I gather that that was quite a shock to you," he then says, certainly wary, not matter-of-factly. "Did it awaken memories of that war?"

Again, she nods.

"I am sorry," he says, "that was not the intention." For a while there's just their footsteps down the hallway, the other hospital sounds, and the light streaming through doors and windows. Just before he opens his office door, he speaks again: "Unfortunately, I don't know enough about that war. I am a physician, I was never a professional soldier. And like most of us, I tried to forget everything I knew about that war as quickly as possible."

She follows him into his office like a somnambulant, swaying slightly. She sits down and looks at the large window behind him, at the leaves rustling quietly, at an insect – a dragonfly? – that briefly reflects the sunlight, a brilliant white spark. Funny how one can be completely cut off from the light, as if there is nothing else outside, nothing except the darkness within.

She looks at Hurst, who is watching her from his chair. When their eyes meet he smiles, albeit briefly, but he has evidently noticed that her dismay is waning.

She holds his gaze for a while, preoccupied, before she speaks. "The music ..." She drops her head so that her left cheek rests on the outstretched fingers of her left hand. "That's what we'd last spoken about, not so? You might find it strange, but yes, my music programme does to some extent come from that war, the one in South Africa, I mean. What I mean is that it is based on my memories.

"It's a long story; in fact, it's in and of itself *the* story." She realises that she's starting to sound incoherent, that she's touching on things that she doesn't actually want to articulate; she sits up straight and speaks with studied determination: "It's a story – you could call it a folk tale – that I'd heard … and that's the story behind my whole thing with music." She falls silent, as if she is listening to something, and then starts again: "It's a story … that someone told, someone told me." She sees Hurst lift a finger to his mouth almost cautiously, and her immediate reaction is to try to explain herself, to justify her clarification by appealing to Rivers, but something – yes, there's an apprehensiveness that she notices in Hurst – which makes her hesitate, and then she abandons the explanation and says somewhat distantly and monotonously: "It's a tale of two brothers. It comes from the stories of the people of Lesotho, and in them, I mean in the stories, all sorts of things are possible, like people who can turn into animals and then become human again, that sort of thing. Now, in this story the older brother murders the younger one in order to get his inheritance. The murdered brother then changes into a singing bird that keeps circling the head of the murderer."

"A murder story?" Hurst's mouth is a slanted, sceptical stripe.

She hears the chorus in Tiisetso's story: *Tsoei-lee, tsoei-lee, tsoei-lee* … Masilo chopped up Masilonyane at the fountain. He wants the dappled cow that walks among the white ones. *Tsoei-lee, tsoei-lee, tsoei-lee* … Why on earth did she bring this up? She sees Hurst's searching eyes, the meerkat eyes. She'll have to explain, she knows that. To herself, too. She says: "It's an African thing. Traditional medicine. Primitive people …" Would he understand anything whatsoever?

"This is a story that you heard from these primitive people?" His voice is soft, measured. No, she was wrong, there is nothing sceptical about him. But what would the story mean to him? It is senseless to bring it up here, in this hospital, in this country. The story is completely incomprehensible here, you cannot tell it here. It's a story that should simply hang like smoke over a dung fire on red soil hardened by bare feet.

But she just nods her head. "I'm sure you know what I mean." She looks at him expectantly for a few seconds, then explains: "That, as with songs, one can arrive at the source of one's healing through stories. And that healing and harm can often not be distinguished from one another."

He looks down and wipes something off the desk. "If you can find a story that matters, one that you both believe, that has meaning for both of you, then yes. And the ambivalence, the sort you're referring to, is surely a characteristic of any meaningful story."

"I know," she says feebly. She'd hardly been listening to him; indeed, as she herself was talking she'd begun to wonder why she'd brought up Tiisetso's story. Why this story specifically, which she thought she'd forgotten long ago, and one about primitive instincts and eternal guilt?

She tried to puzzle through it. She and Hurst are sitting here. In front of her lies the folder that he'd given her, the patient folder. That patient is lying in a room somewhere in this hospital.

To the left of Hurst's shoulder is the window with its grasping branches and clouds with whiskered cheeks. She gets up quickly. Something is beginning to filter through …

yes, she thinks she now knows. She presses Hamilton-Peake's folder against her chest, but almost immediately rips it away. The knowledge lifts its head like a snake: She has been lying to Hurst all along. Also to herself. The healing power of stories is the last thing that she had in mind. Hurst's conclusion was right on the mark: She is thinking about murder.

Chapter 18

It's what I do most of the time, sit in the sun like this with the warm rock under my legs. That, and looking for food for the meerkat. Crickets. Scorpions. Worms. In the beginning I managed to hold down a scorpion's tail with a twig and then somehow cut it off like this, but I soon saw that the meerkat knows itself how to catch a scorpion. Or a gecko. Probably a snake too if we could find one. He accompanies me on hunting expeditions, turns rocks over, searches in the grass. Not too far away, just around the cave here and then back again, he and I.

My legs have turned brown from baking in the sun. How many days have I been sitting here like this? A few weeks already, at the very least. The days come and go, one like the next. In the camp I showed Alice how to get rid of leg hairs by making a cord from tail hairs of a horse and rubbing this up and down her calves and shins. Our nursemaid taught me this. Thuleka was her name, but we called her Sannie.

I wonder where Thuleka is now. She and Tsela. That sly rubbish. It is him who went and told them that we were burying the household goods. He brought the English. He and someone else, I can't remember now, but the two of them brought the English. I was still digging with the spade because

Ma was too tired by now and when I looked up again, they were standing there. Two Englishmen and a man, and that Tsela, who'd worked for Uncle Thys for heaven knows how many years, long before we even arrived. Ma and I just stood there and neither of us could say anything. I think I was too shocked.

They must have come through the bluegums, that's why we didn't hear them. Ma had said that morning that the soil at the anthills below the ridge was deep and soft enough.

Now it's all coming back to me, all these things that happened. When I sit like this and watch. It comes to me like the commandos I sometimes see trekking past. At first it's just dust kicked up on the horizon and then the horses' hooves become longer and longer until they look like giraffes struggling to get through the thin air. Sometimes smoke. Black smoke that rises slowly. But everything is far away and then the wind blows it all away again.

The other man who was there where Ma and I were digging, he laughed and said it looked to him as if we didn't want to listen. He spoke Afrikaans. He had a way of hitching his pants up with both hands on either side of his belt buckle. I just cannot remember his face, or his name. There were so many things that happened. Ma had looked around and down at the things that we wanted to bury. The dinner service with the delicate intertwining flowers that she'd inherited from Ouma. A big meat platter and the soup tureen and six plates. The cutlery was already wrapped in a flour sack, but it also lay there.

The one Englishman said they would send a wagon the next day to come and fetch us, and then they all went back through the bluegums again. This time I could see them going through the trees, actually, just their shadows. After a while, the sound of the horses' hooves. Ma just sat on the ground.

I think I knew then that it was our last day on the farm. I tried to look at everything in such a way that I would never forget it, but now I have half-forgotten. Neels is alone at the house, Ma said after a long while, and I helped her up. She was already battling to walk then.

Sometimes when I sit like this, the meerkat comes out of the nest I made for him from a paraffin can. Tiisetso had brought the can. He is continually bringing things. The meerkat comes to me with these stiff little paws and his nose to the ground. He does not go away, he stays with me. He is my meerkat.

I actually have a lot of time to think here, because the things that I remember do not make me feel good. And I want to get better. I want to get all the pain and the stiffness out of my body. At least I'm now praying, in the morning and in the evening, on my knees. Tiisetso and Mamello can stare all they want. They must just look. If only I had a Bible, then I could read to them too. I say some of the verses as I remember them: Or the golden bowl be broken, or the pitcher be broken at the fountain, or the wheel broken at the cistern.

Tiisetso burns some twigs and grass on what looks like a ploughshare, it could even be bomb shrapnel, and then he puts it next to me at night. In the beginning I said that it stank, but he says it is *meriane* – medicine. He says I must follow the cattle of the *badimo* – the old people who have already died. I think I know what he means. I am beginning to understand him bit by bit. He's also given me a mirror. The mirror and the knife and the fork he picked up where the

English burned down Uncle Jan Gildenhuis's house. I asked him what he was looking for there.

I asked him if he helped to burn down the house. I screamed and threw sand at him, but Tiisetso just kept standing there. With his face turned away.

I'm sorry that I spoke to Tiisetso like that, but I cannot face looking into the mirror yet. It's lying around in the back of the cave somewhere. Through a glass darkly. The Lord must first forgive me, take the sin away from me. I have sinned terribly, I know that, and if I look into that mirror now it will only make me more ill. And I cannot get worse, because then I'll die. Here, in this cave, with these people, is the only place where I can get better.

Chapter 19

Colonel H.A. Hamilton-Peake. Her eyes move from letter to letter; it's as if she can see the tiny grooves that the pen has etched into the paper. She opens the file. Is it possible that there is someone else with that name? *Statement of the services of no. 148079.* And then that name in cursive. Thick ink lines. Below that, the service record in columns under different headings. The entries were made in writing that is practically illegible. The paper soiled by handling. She turns the page, similar entries in columns. Then there is a description of him at the time of his recruitment. He was eighteen years and three months old when he signed up, five feet eight inches tall, one hundred and forty pounds. It says there that his complexion is medium, his eyes dark grey, hair light brown. It's him.

She pages back again and looks for familiar words, for phrases that, in anticipation, fill her with a paralysing fear. And then, almost unnoticed, it slips into her consciousness, her whole being set like a trap to catch it, and as it registers it is as if she's been battling with it for a while already: *South Africa.* He's there after all. It's him. At first she just sits, stunned and blinded, before feverishly searching further. What for, she does not know. He's received the Queen's South Africa Medal, she sees. And the King's. Then he must have been in South Africa until the end of the war. He came from Littabourne, Pilton, Barnstaple, Devon. She knows the region well enough by now to know that it's not too far from Newton Abbot.

She flicks quickly to get to the last pages in the file. The final service report details his collapse and hysterical episode during an offensive in Flanders, where he was a supply officer in the artillery corps. His treatment report indicates that he suffers from insomnia, hysterical episodes and is constantly threatening suicide. Somewhat sceptically, someone added in quotation marks: *"if he can't have his own way"*. Every Monday, Wednesday and Friday he is sprayed with a high-pressure hose before being put into a warm bath for an hour to relax his muscles for the exercises in the officers' recreation hall. With little success, reads the entry. He has been in the hospital for four months already.

Hurst must therefore have known that they both come from South Africa. What exactly does he have in mind? Does he know more, did Hamilton-Peake let something slip? She closes the file and gets up.

Susan knocks softly on Hurst's door, sticks her head in after he answers. "I just wanted to say that I'll walk home this afternoon," she says.

"Alone?"

She shrugs.

"Let Jacobs go with you," he says. "These days there're mainly scoundrels loitering around – all the good men are at the front." He sits back. "Have you looked at the folder?"

"That's why I want to walk. Gives me time to reflect."

He nods, and she pulls the door closed. Somewhat startled by the click of the lock. Her legs are lame, her stomach is in a knot. She is intensely aware of her footsteps on the wooden floor, tries to focus on that, seeking reassurance from the clacking of her soles that it is she walking, that she is walking on this earth and not floating loose through the ether. The cool air is now in her face; the grey sky is thickening above the rolling hills. The road is wedged between thick shrubbery – brambles, she thinks, though she's not at all certain, obviously not kwarrie, what on earth is she thinking, it's England after all, it's not … She tries to concentrate her thoughts, but they flap about, like frightened birds trapped in a tent, fluttering against the dirty white tarpaulin, casting grotesque shadows above the lamp.

Again she hears her footsteps, muted now. The ground is soggy, her footsteps heavier, more intense. Has she been sent here? Was it fate that they'd cross paths again? It had happened sixteen years ago. Warm. The night sky shot to smithereens. She is stepping through the tent ropes. Behind her is Alice's wheezing, in her mind the face covered in sweat, the blood in the corners of the mouth. She stumbles over something, and then the voice and the grasping of her arm, the breath against her cheek. The dull glow on a face, the moving of a mouth below a moustache. She tries to pull free, but her arm is a slender branch in a gnarled fist.

She walks faster. Her breathing begins to race. She looks around, just the dark empty road, the bushes, the trees, and the musty smell of grain. She starts running, her dress restricting her legs, her shoes chafing. Every so often she stumbles. Her gaze fixed on the road ahead, from the corners of her eyes the bushes flit by, the first houses look down from the heights. She gathers her dress and runs, stumbles, zig-zags across the road, regains her balance and then runs with swinging arms towards the house that waits farther down the street.

And then she comes to a halt.

What's got into her? She looks back at the empty street. There is nothing. What on earth has got into her? She waits for her panting to slow, tries to retrieve something coherent from the fluttering in her thoughts, but finds only that, nothing else, only the fluttering.

She walks the last stretch in a focused and measured way. As she knocks on the door she's fairly certain that the last trace of terror is gone. The afternoon shade would have returned her normal colour to her face, the sweat she has wiped away, her breathing has steadied, her gaze is firm.

She remains standing in the twilight entrance hall until Mrs Simms has locked the door behind them. Usually she waits out of courtesy, but today she is wary of the loneliness of her room, making her stand around in the hall, somewhat irritated by her own neediness.

"My goodness, Susan," Mrs Simms says with a swishing hem, "you look like you've just seen a German."

She feels the annoyance bubbling up inside her uncontrollably. She turns her face away from the irksome old woman. Touches her cheek as if trying to ascertain what has been written so clearly and visibly on her face.

"Come," the old woman clucks, "let me make us both a

138

cup of tea. I'm sure there are things you experience at that hospital ... a hellish place, I tell you."

She follows the mumbling woman shuffling off in front of her. She stares at the seams of the blouse, the low bun that hops and bobs on the collar. Below the blouse, layers of protective, supportive cotton.

Cotton that shifts and wrinkles over the soft flesh that bulges like dough over the interlocking fists of the corset. And then the image is in her head: her mother kneading the dough with a consuming fury, with pummelling fists, and Mrs Simms wriggling as she helplessly tries to ward off pale fists, bending her head back in a final attempt to face the onslaught. Then Susan bumps into Mrs Simms, and she struggles wildly to undo the collision, to recoil from her touch. What particularly upsets Susan is that Mrs Simms has looked around at her in the exact same way she'd just seen in the onslaught of her mother's fists. She goes and sits at the table, hears the woman busying herself, not daring to look at that bundle of motherliness in lace and cotton. Nothing interrupts this train of thought; she seems to be passive in the face of this offensive arising from deep within.

"We all have days like this," says the old woman.

If only we could fight against it, thought Susan. And not just stand by, passively watching. She puts a hand to her throat, feels the pulse, her breath against her skin. She takes her hand away quickly, placing both elbows on the table. If only we had not stood and watched as everything was burned down around us, our furniture, our pantry shelves, our bedding, our cupboards being emptied, stood and watched as feathers and ash whirled over the yard that we had smoothed and swept so that it lay like an open palm under the house. Under us. And then she hears herself speak, her voice a ball of warm breath in the hollow formed by her lowered head and arms above the table top.

"Perhaps the only option is that we also go to the front," she says, and looks up.

"We?" The woman turns around, looking at her with wide eyes as if she has finally found the object of her daily scanning of the air.

"We women," says Susan. "Go and fight with guns and bayonets and … and God knows what else it is that men use … to get everything over and done with instead of this effort to try to maintain the place on their behalf."

She realises that she has lost control of her voice. Mrs Simms's wide-eyed gaze is still fixed on her, her gaping mouth a rosy stain, her teeth visible. Mrs Simms laughs, seemingly amused. She bares her teeth like a tiny predator. Two predators at the table, Susan thinks, and she feels relief wash over her, inexplicable and just as unexpected as her previous perception of the softly bulging, wrinkled skin of a kind, motherly, nurturing woman.

Chapter 20

Tiisetso walks ahead and I follow, slipping and sliding behind him. He has a long stick in one hand, slim and delicate as the feeler of a cricket, and a bright blue blanket around his shoulders. I have to keep lifting up my black dress so that it doesn't drag on the ground, but it's easier now that I have shoes, even though they're a bit too big for me. It is still pitch-dark; it must be very early, as I hardly slept for more than an hour.

Last night Tiisetso arrived at the fire wearing different clothes, if one could call them clothes. He wore a sort of overcoat made of dassie and lynx hide – with the tails as tassels. He was wearing all his bracelets, and he had his knobkerrie and *lesiba* with him, but he also had a string of beads around his head, with feathers dangling over an ear. I got quite a fright when I saw him.

Mamello just kept stoking the fire, and then she stood up and I heard her walk down to wherever it was that they lived. I had never seen their house. Tiisetso played the *lesiba*, and after a while Mamello came back, also wearing different clothes. At least her skirt was made from fabric, but above that she only wore strings of beads that hung from her shoulders over her chest. Nothing else. She had two pillowslips with her, one in each hand. There was a live creature in the one, I saw it move and it also made noises.

Mamello put the pillowslips on the ground, the one with the thing inside was tied with a knot.

She began to sing and Tiisetso played and Mamello danced and jerked her shoulders forward, turning her head from side to side and clapping her hands. They sang and sang and sang, and then I stood up, because I had already done that a lot. I knew it so well that I could sing along, and I also started shaking my shoulders like Mamello – and by now I could do it without any pain. When I first did this it used to hurt, and I also laughed a lot, so much so that Mamello also started laughing.

We sang of horses walking clipitty-swish through water and cattle growing fat in the long grass and children calling their mothers and we sang and sang until the stars sank down and joined us in the cave and we became part of the night. They danced close to me, right next to me. We danced in a circle around the fire, our feet shuffled over the stones, sh-sh-sh, and many things came into my head and then flew out again. Ma and Neels were also in my head, and I was quite surprised by that, as if they were people I'd seen for the very first time. We were in the tent, I was with Ma, and the tent was drawn closed and baked warm by the sun and on the bed was Neels covered in all our blankets with just his little head sticking out and quietly looking at Ma and me with his big blue eyes. There was a thread hanging from Ma's sleeve where the seam meets the shoulder, and when Ma also died, three months later, I searched for that thread, I wanted to break it off for her but I couldn't find it, and Ma just lay there so quietly.

Sh-sh-sh, we dance, jerre-jerre-jerre, and Tiisetso goes and squats on the ground, and Mamello too and I kneel next to her. We crouch in front of Tiisetso and he keeps blowing on his *lesiba* and rocks his upper body to and fro, to and fro, and the night with all its stars encircles us, enfolds us.

Mamello takes the one pillowslip and unties the knot. It's a guinea fowl; he kicks wildly and flaps his wings and starts screeching; his eyes shine in the firelight, his helmet blue, his soldier's helmet a deep blue, the flames darting through the cave making it seem that there are many people with us, dancing around us. I feel myself coming closer and closer to something, something in the dark that I cannot yet see, and Mamello pushes the guinea fowl against the stones and takes a knife from her pocket, she thrusts the blade in under the guinea fowl's neck feathers and the bird screams and the blood spurts and I taste the blood in my mouth, it is in my eyes and I am being dragged by the leg between the tents and shoved into the camp supervisor's brightly lit tent, and at the table are two Khakis, I know them, I see them every day, and Krisjan Schutte the joiner shouts here she is, the camp whore, here she is and he throws me down on the floor, and one of the Khakis grabs me by the hair and pulls me up, and I grab at his jacket and a button, a gold button comes off and rolls onto the tarpaulin and Schutte falls to his knees to pick it up, and the three of them, Schutte and the two Khakis, pin me to the bed and they pull my dress up and over my head so that I cannot see anything and now I know what they are going to do, I know what they are going to do and I feel it before it actually happens and I pull my head out from under my dress and what they are doing I have not learnt the words for yet, I cannot say it, the blood on my face and in my mouth and the night and the stars around us and Mamello plucks the guinea fowl clean and we braai it on the coals, the open fire, the flames, we break bits off and push them into our mouths and we taste the flesh, the tough, succulent flesh, and our mouths chew as one, we breathe, we are alive, and it's as if the whole night beats in unison with my heart, thud-thudding, beating with my heart.

I had not even noticed that Tiisetso had stopped playing, but when I looked again Mamello was speaking to me. Ntauleng, my child, she said, *ngwana ya hesu* – you are our child. We slaughtered for you, because you are the one who changes the clouds, you are the one who flies low over the ground with the little birds, your heart walks far, far, far, far, your heart walks far. She closed her eyes when she spoke, she clapped with one hand onto her other palm. She said that the time had come for them to put me out onto the road. There is a road that I must walk, she said, because I am the one who can see far ahead because I have come out of darkness. I sat quietly and listened to her, the singing was not in vain. Then she said I must go to Bloemfontein, there is a coach going tomorrow and Tiisetso has spoken to that driver, and I can go along.

I listened to Mamello, but looked at the can where the meerkat slept. I pulled my legs up and felt my heart beat against my thighs. I looked at the can and did not want to look up. I am leaving.

144

Mamello took clothes from the pillowslip, the black dress with the long sleeves and the frilled collar, a black bonnet and shoes. She showed me that there were more clothes in the slip, and a loaf of bread wrapped in cloth. I must not be scared, she said to me, *e tla e o supisa* – it will be shown to you. I looked at Tiisetso. Is this so? I asked him. His head dropped low onto his chest. Yes, he said. He knows a man who works in Balla Bosiu, he's one of the Scouts. He's the one who will be taking the coach down to Bloemfontein. He held out his hand to Mamello and she put a tobacco pouch in it. Then he stood up and held the pouch out to me, his left hand supporting his right forearm, as is their custom. *Tjhelete*, he said.

I took the money and put it in my pocket. What about the meerkat? I asked, though I already knew that there was no other way. I can't spend my whole life in that cave, and I am now well enough. But I was scared. I started shaking. And I would need a pass. What if they asked for my pass? What about the meerkat? I asked again.

We will look after him, Mamello said. We will look at him, and we'll know whether you are well.

Where am I going? Back to the camp?

Mamello put the blanket around me and made me lie down. She said I was going away to Mangaung, to Bloemfontein. She said I must say that I am a *Monyesemane*, that I am English. She said that they would wake me early. They had spoken to the driver of the coach; he would give me a pass.

She and Tiisetso stayed next to the fire, sitting up and at a distance from each other. They just kept sitting quietly like that. And I lay watching them and thought about what I would say if the Khakis asked for my pass, and I saw that the night with all its stars had left the cave, but I was both happy and sad. I looked at Tiisetso and Mamello and I was no longer scared. I was happy and I was sad.

Now I am following Tiisetso. I actually know the way to town, all along the stream and then there is a footpath that is a trampled strip, past the location, and once you get to the first houses then it is easy to find the hotel. That is where the coach will be waiting. I follow the dark shape that must be Tiisetso, follow the sound of his shoes on the stones, the grass and the bushes against his trousers. I know we will soon be hearing the coughing and crying coming from the camp and I keep my eyes on the ground, tread carefully, because the one thing I still see more clearly than anything, even with my eyes shut tight, are the rows of white tents against the black trampled veld.

At the location the dogs are barking. The town is quiet. We walk across the square, but I don't look at the morgue tent. The coach stands in front of the hotel, with eight horses in harness. The harnesses creak. There is a man with a broad-brimmed hat standing next to the coach. He has a gun slung over his shoulder, and I know he is the Scout.

When Tiisetso comes to a halt, I also stop. The man at the coach says something. Tiisetso turns in my direction, and my legs walk past him as if of their own volition. The man opens the door.

You must go well, Ntauleng, Tiisetso says. He gives me the pillowslip with the clothes and bread that he has been carrying. I sit down and the door closes. I sit in the dark coach and

146

take a deep breath so as not to cry. Once I've exhaled and sat quietly for a while, I realise that there are also other people in the coach. I take another deep breath and hold it in for so long that it feels as if I am about to explode like a bomb.

Chapter 21

She lies on her back, her eyes open wide, only vaguely aware of the stuffy room in which the outlines of the chest of drawers and the mirror, the lamp on its spiral stand of dark wood, the listless curtains, are all melting into one in the growing dusk. She listens carefully to the faint creak of the bed as she breathes, looks with equal concentration at the light still glimmering behind the lace curtain. She lies, stiff as a post. In expectation. Something is going to happen any moment now. Initially this afternoon's outburst towards Mrs Simms, so utterly senseless, kept churning through her mind, but eventually she realised that her anxiety has to do with something very specific. And it comes from elsewhere, has nothing to do with the hospital or Mrs Simms or ... she lies and listens, yes. And almost immediately after this realisation it dawns on her that she is waiting for the roar of an approaching plane! How long has she known? How long has she known that it would come? That, twisting, it would break through the clouds and that the pilot would lean out and that she would recognise his face just before he ...

She gives a start as someone knocks on the door. "Susan ..."

It is Mrs Simms.

She does not move. Anxiety sits like a cat on her chest.

148

Then she hears the woman mumbling and footsteps dying down along the passage.

She swings her legs off the bed, carefully sits up.

She remains sitting, almost transfixed. It happens occasionally, this worry about a possible bombing. It is an anxiety she has known since ... oh, ever since she can remember. The knock at the door has at least released her from the grip of this oppressive feeling, yet something still hovers, something that lies just beyond the borders of certainty. A knock at the door. A dark room. Bikes clattering across cobbles. A woman calling out. Calling in Dutch.

Then she knows. It's her apartment in Dordrecht. Those evenings she waited on her bed or in a chair or next to the drawn curtains, waiting for Jacques to stop knocking on her door.

It is Jacques.

Before the war his face was open and clear, wide-eyed, his chin cleft symmetrically like a shiny pumpkin. That was before France needed him. Before he came to say goodbye, half-elated with a shy smile.

And when he returned from the front, it was in a uniform that looked as if it had been woven from dog hair and a moustache that hid his mouth like buffalo horns.

Suddenly he was there again one day, on the stairs, just like before.

Just like the time when he used to pedal his bike to the Johann de Witt gymnasium on weekdays, slowly and with his back straight and knees bent as behoves a teacher, with a Latin reader in a leather satchel on his carrier. But now, with him standing half-stricken behind his moustache, she's had to look twice. And she remembered with a shock, or rather a sort of mortifying excitement, the time she told him about Aunt Marie introducing her to a man. He'd sat and listened with the fingers of both hands around a glass of gin, head held low, like a calf cornered in an enclosure, how he'd moved his head around awkwardly as if his collar was throttling him, and she told him about the moustached man who arrived with his calling card, and it felt to her as if something like ink was running down the corners of her mouth, down her throat, into her collar, down between her breasts, and she tasted power, how she could banish with one breath that jellied blob of fear that she was when the man knocked at the door, and she threw it into Jacques's face: Look, I stood there, and his moustache shook with desire for me, he wanted me. And she saw Jacques withering in the heat of her story, in the face of her capacity to create her own world, to be its omniscient author.

And here he was again, a moustached soldier on a staircase. "You're back?" she said.

He just shrugged and leant with his back against the wall so that she could pass by. After she unlocked her door she realised that he was behind her. She turned around and it was then, at her door, with just the two of them in the dimly lit hall stretching away from them on either side, that she saw the desperate desire in his eyes. Her handbag to her chest, she felt for the door with her left hand behind her. She looked at his pleading eyes – the darting eyeballs, the contraction, the kaleidoscope of brown in his irises.

She had opened the door behind her, stepping in back-wards, and she could not take her eyes off him. It was as if what she'd seen there had unravelled between them like an umbilical cord. He followed her in and she indicated that he should sit at the table. She had a bottle of gin in her cupboard, and when she reached for it her hand shook uncontrollably. She took hold of the bottle and thought: I am seeing a dying man. He did not look at her; his hands were like dead birds on the table. And she stood there in the terrible, wonderful presence of a man whose spirit was already dribbling away in bloody droplets into a trench rank with male fear.

Only later, when he had left for the front again, did she wonder how she could have known it all. How she could have known that about him. He did not speak; he could not speak. He took small sips of his gin and spoke haltingly, un-certain and searching for words about ... what, exactly? It was something he remembered from his early childhood, she remembers now, how he'd walked home hand in hand with his mother from the park. Something like that.

She sat quietly and listened to him, noticing how his hands balled into fists that could explode at any moment and blow them both to bits, and she wanted to reach out and squeeze his ear, feel the warm elasticity of the cartilage between her fingers, and she knew that the sensation would make his whole body break out in a fine sweat, especially the tender white skin of his armpits and lower down at the slight bulge over his hipbone, down to the turned-over black soil of his loins.

But she did not. She kept clutching the glass, her eyes fixed on the shimmering motion of the liquid as it swirled round and round, and she watched helplessly as she and Jacques and their whole world flattened out to that invisibly thin taut membrane, to the transparent, shapeless, complete and utter inscrutability of water in a glass.

She is lying on her bed again, as taut as a string, her thoughts entangled in memories of her and Jacques in that room that grew steadily colder. She lies there a long time, beyond help, and then something starts taking shape inside her. It's as if she were once again opening the door to her apartment in Dordrecht, opening the door hesitantly and peering into the half-light. This time she sees herself sitting there with the soldier. She looks at herself. And only now, from this distance, can she see that she'd sat at that table waiting, sat with the glass in her hand, frozen with fear, waiting for him to see through her, for him to peer right into her wretched whore's heart, to see and to *know*.

Eventually she falls asleep in her clothes on top of the bedding. Restless; keeps waking from a dream. At one stage she hears the intermittent tolling of a church bell. In her dream she is much younger and is standing barefoot in a dirty cotton frock in a bell tent. Her mother is also in the dream, and their shadows are large and distorted against the sides of the tent. Her mother throws a pair of her father's old work trousers onto the bed, the pair that makes little horns at the back where the suspenders are attached. Her mother tells her to put on the trousers, and she reels back afraid, and at the tent opening is her mother's pale dying face.

She startles awake. It is night. She sits up straight in her bed. She cannot sleep on this bed. She must do something, she must get away. And above all she must get away from her-self, from being captive to her own thoughts.

She puts on a jacket, walks down the hall in her socks, puts on her shoes at the front door. Takes a key off the hook and goes outside.

Chapter 22

There's a slight jerk; it's probably the driver, climbing up onto the coach. I can see very little, and sometimes I think I'm imagining a hand being raised, or the sound of breathing, and I almost die of fright when a male voice suddenly speaks, not far from me on the same seat.

"Perry?"

"Yes, Dr Molesworth." Another man, across from us.

I now know who is sitting next to me. One of the English doctors from the camp, Dr Molesworth. He says: "For a moment I thought you'd got out, but if I am not mistaken, I think we are now honoured by the presence of a lady."

My heart beats, my breathing is too loud. I am thinking about Tiisetso walking back across the dark veld, his long stick scratching at the sky that might be turning blue already. He is going back to the cave, or to where Mamello is waiting at their home. I am going to a place I do not know, but perhaps somewhere, if I'm lucky, that will give me the chance to start afresh.

The man across from me speaks, the one named Perry, he speaks with a younger voice: "Indeed, Doctor. The driver told me there would be three passengers, including a young lady.

Indeed, without a chaperone." And then it sounds as if he is speaking to me: "Excuse me, young lady, but the driver led me to understand that these were unusual circumstances. Not that the circumstance of war is not already unusual enough. But here in the dark it is difficult for me – for us – to introduce ourselves properly."

I hope he can see me nodding from the movement of my bonnet against the curtain. Luckily the coach is shaking so much as it moves off, and the driver is shouting so loudly at the horses, that it's not really necessary to speak. For a while at least we are able to just sit and listen to the clattering of the carriage and the groaning of the wheels.

When the doctor speaks again it is fortunately not to me. He asks Perry if he's seen what he'd wished to see, and at first I think he's asking if he can see *me*, as if he were trying to ascertain who I was, but when Perry speaks I realise he is referring to photographs he'd taken in the camp at Winburg.

It was there, in that camp, that I'd first seen a photograph, and saw how people took photographs. I saw the Van Tonders standing in front of their tent, I remember them borrowing a bed from one of the other tents, and wearing their Sunday best for the man who came to take the pictures. They arranged themselves into a group, and he looked at them through his camera. The youngest Van Tonder was probably about three years old. A few weeks later he was dead. After a while, the same man returned and gave them the picture. That was the first photograph I'd ever seen. In it, the little Van Tonder was still alive.

Dr Molesworth and Perry converse, I just sit and listen. I

think Perry is one of the people who take photographs of the war. The doctor tells Perry why he needs to go to Bloemfontein. It has something to do with the Show Grounds camp and the women they lock up there. They call it the ewe camp. One old woman they took there banged her hands against the corrugated iron for a very long time. They caught her wandering around the tents, to and fro, as if she were looking for something she had dropped on the ground. She walked around like that for a whole day. I remember it well. How she gradually grew quieter, until she stopped speaking altogether and started dying.

Slowly the light filters into the coach. I can't see the doctor, my bonnet is in the way, but sometimes I steal a glance at the man across from me. At Perry. His shoes are shiny, with pointed tips, almost like mine, only shinier. Black trousers, black waistcoat with a watch chain. White shirt and a dark beard that comes to a point on his white shirt. He is looking at me, I know that. When it is light enough, will he speak to me? He will, and what am I going to say? In English?

I don't know how it happened, or where it's come from, but eventually I just have to look at him, at the round spectacles with the thin frame. His eyes are not unfriendly, not at all, and I think his mouth might be laughing under his beard and moustache, I don't know, but he nods and says good morning. He says his name is Jack Perry. And then it just slips out: Susan, I say, Susan Draper. And my voice is so hoarse that it gives me a fright and I clutch my throat to indicate that it hurts, and then I look at the man to the left of me, the older one, the doctor, and he just looks at me silently

156

with his tired, watery blue eyes and he nods and says pleased to meet you.

That's all. Then we just sit there. Later Jack Perry draws the curtains on his side and I see the bare veld shimmering in the morning sun, and I think about what I had said to them, that I had taken Alice's surname, and that Alice was probably dead by now.

It was me and Hester Cloete and Joey Luwes who kept vigil at Alice Draper's bed that night. The other three who stayed with us in the tents were at the English party, they were celebrating New Year. Everyone should have been there, but we stayed behind. In tent number 19. The young women's tent. Alice began moaning, a big drum began to beat beat beat at the festivities and then the screech of a bagpipe with the rattatatta of a smaller drum. Not far from us a baby was crying and we could clearly hear the mother's shh-shh.

That is what I sit thinking in the coach as dawn approaches. Then through the window I see two horses, then the tent and then a few Khakis in front of the tent. Two of them are standing, the others sit and watch us. The Scout on the box shouts whoa! ... whoa! And the coach comes to a halt.

Even if I'd wanted to get out, I can't, my legs are too weak. Perry opens the door and lets the doctor alight first. Then he climbs down and holds a hand out to me. I cannot do otherwise, and his hand feels so warm under mine. As I touch the ground I lift my dress and walk quickly, then I run. There are a few thorn trees and reeds, as well as long grass. There is a pool there, at the reeds, and hoof prints in the mud. That's

157

why the English pitched camp here, the water. I look back, but the trees are between me and the coach and the tent and everything they're busy with there.

I don't know how long I have been standing there among the thorn trees.

The sun is already high, and when I walk back to the coach my shadow stretches out in front of me. Perry and Dr Molesworth are already seated. Perry gives me a mug of coffee. I remember to say thank you and to make my voice sound hoarse. Then the doctor sticks his hand into an inside pocket and takes out a flat tin. He opens it and holds it out to me. He says they are lozenges for my throat, and that I should take two.

Before the doctor closes the tin, he takes a piece of metal from between the lozenges and holds it up between a forefinger and thumb for Perry and me to see. It's a longish, slightly bent piece of copper, almost like a finger, though in fact I know what it is. The doctor says it's a Mauser bullet he'd removed from the stomach of a soldier. There's a groove on the side, and he explains it's where the bullet hit a rib before lodging just below the skin of the abdomen.

There is nothing outside. Only the great red sun and the bare veld. Beside me, the doctor is speaking. There is no other sound apart from his voice and the hooves and the coach. The doctor is speaking, and every now and then Perry says something or asks a question. The doctor's voice sounds as if it is being dragged from a rope tied to the coach, dragging in the dust kicked up by the wheels. He tells Perry about soldiers who have been shot. He explains what happens when a bullet hits. A Mauser bullet. At times I steal a glance at the doctor, see how his jaw jumps up and down though his eyes remain quiet and tired, with every now and then a blink so slow that I think they have fallen shut.

The doctor indicates with his finger, as if he were writing on a blackboard. The rim of the hole where the bullet enters is darker, he says, as if stained by the metal. It's almost like the mark you'd see if you shot a bullet through a wad of paper, through a book. But it's a very narrow rim, and if the bullet passed through clothing you wouldn't easily see it; the rim turns navy-blue anyway as a result of the bruising. But then, says the doctor, it doesn't matter how the bullet bruises you, whether it's a thick or thin rim. Sooner or later all bullet holes develop something that looks like a halo. How long afterwards? It's the doctor himself asking, and after a while he answers his question. Yes, it varies, he says, but it comes, it eventually comes. About half an inch thick, after a while it sits there. Like a halo.

I look at Perry's chest as the doctor speaks. A halo, that's what the doctor calls it. And it's only after a while that I realise I've been looking at Perry like that. At the seam of his waistcoat, at how his fingers must have pushed the buttons through the buttonholes, and I see how the fabric of his jacket rises and falls with his breathing. Then I suddenly feel sick with anxiety. And my eyes go up and up, and perhaps Perry's beard trembles, I think so, but his mouth is slightly agape above his beard and his eyes look straight at me, and look at me sharply, and he sees how my hands grab my dress in front of me, and I don't know why, but it really feels to me as if that hole that a bullet makes, that halo the doctor spoke of, is something that you can never ever hide. Perry also knows that, I think. He knows that you can never hide it.

Chapter 23

The night is cool, damp. Street lights. The rattle of wheels in the distance. Voices. A lone woman, but still, she'll do it. No one can stop her now.

It's not too far, The Sphinx. After Jacobs showed it to her that first day she's noticed it daily on her way to the hospital. It's where the hospital staff get together. The women too. "Are you coming?" one of them once asked during teatime with a provoking look, as if it were a kind of test. Ten years ago it would have been a challenge that she might have accepted. Once or twice she'd been with Jacques to a café – that's what they're called in the Netherlands. Here, the girls at the hospital say, you must simply ensure that there is more than one woman in the group, then it is acceptable, highly acceptable, one of them babbled and they all burst out laughing.

Things have changed since the war. It is a pretty war, lovely, this British one; you cannot imagine a lovelier war. Her shoes flash under the streetlamps; her shadow bleeds out before her. To the left is a long white wall, to the fore a suspended signboard, then the door with its heavy dark wood.

She hears voices behind it, pushes the door open with her shoulder, and when she enters the raucous half-lit space, she knows that this is exactly what she's come for: the smell, the presence of male bodies, the heaviness, the solidity that contrasts with her own gliding weightlessness.

A moment later she stands dazed and blinded, as if a bomb has exploded in front of her. When the bombs explode you become light-headed, one of the men in a hospital bed had told her, a captain, but it's what you've been trained for. You don't feel scared, you feel excited. In a way, it's like the thoroughbreds in the Grand National: round and round they gallop, clearing every obstacle, some fall down and don't get up again, others persevere to the bitter end. To the bitter end.

Then she sees the table closest to the door, three or four women, they're sitting looking at her over their glasses, one of them is Anne Maxwell. She quickly looks away, searching the room filled with men, the light from the bulbs filtering through swirls of smoke onto heads and shoulders. She had thought – or hoped, rather – that she'd see Anne here, the one condition, in fact, upon which she would enter this man's world. Alone she could not do it. A lone woman. Whore!

She pulls her gaze from the men, searches for Anne's eyes. Anne pulls her head back, her chin lowered, lips pouting in mock surprise. Come, she gestures, come and sit down. She joins them, and the other women sit back in their chairs for the introductions. Full of smiles. Susan leans forward. What's so funny? She peers intently at the faces. "They think I'm funny," says Anne.

"You are very, very funny," one of them says and they burst out laughing.

"Just telling them a bit about my work," Anne says, cool

as ever, although to Susan it seems that there's a faint glow on her cheeks and her breath is lightly racing.

"About the people we work with," Anne says. "You'd know, not so? I've already shown them everything. Convulsions? A spastic walk? Fish flaps?" She makes slow flapping movements with her hand.

She's mimicking the patients! She's making fun of them. Susan manages a smile but looks away uncomfortably. What on earth is she supposed to do? The one thing Reymaker taught her is that you do not make fun of it all. Psychiatry is a serious matter. But then ... she snorts. It's as if the very thought of Reymaker was the catalyst. The serious, highly respected figure of authority, filled daily with only the purest of motives. She looks up from her hands. Sees Anne watching her enquiringly, but she's completely cool-headed. Reckless.

"Maybe it'll help if I have something to drink," Susan says. What does one drink here? Beer? In Dordrecht, with Jacques, she sometimes asked for a sherry. Is that permissible? She looks at the other women's glasses. It might as well be water.

"Ask Jacobs," Anne says. "He's also here. We should try to get his attention."

"Don't worry, I'll go and look for him," Susan says and gets up immediately, only too relieved to get away.

Jacobs is seated at the counter, in uniform, listening to an old man standing at his side. She manoeuvers in next to him, careful not to touch him. From the movement of his head, the way he seems to want to turn around, she guesses that he is aware of her. It's rather exciting, this cunning of hers.

At first he glances to the side and then he registers and completely overreacts, as if something has frightened him. "Sister Nell!" he shouts. "For a moment I thought you were the witch of Sheepstor," he laughs loudly, his mouth agape, putting his hand conspiratorially on her shoulder to soften any possible offence. He turns to the old man to introduce Susan, but he has already turned his back, seemingly on the lookout for other company, and Jacobs bends towards her to make himself heard: "One of the ghosts from Crazywell Pool." He's explaining his reference to witches, she knows. "Do you remember? We drove past there at Dartmoor."

She remembers the pool in the middle of nowhere with its water as black as slate. Many years ago, apparently, the congregation of Sheepstor brought the church-bell ropes in an attempt to plumb its depth. With the ropes tied together the bell was let down, but still the bottom could not be reached.

"Is that what you're doing here?" she asks. "Telling ghost stories?"

He shrugs. "What are you drinking?" he asks. "Same as them?" He nods in the direction of Anne and her friends at the door.

"I'll have whatever you're drinking," she says. She supposes it must be beer, the golden liquid in a generous glass.

He gives her a standard smile, looks to see if he can attract the barman's attention, then turns to her again. "And are you still holding out?" he asks. "Or do you feel that you've also got shellshock?"

Again she feels the itch of an irritation that's been lying under her skin for a while now, and while he talks to the barman she looks round at the women who'd yet again burst out laughing.

When he turns to her with the glass of beer she asks: "How did you manage to do your service here and not at the front?"

"Oh," he says, clearly caught unawares. "Oh." He passes the glass to her and lifts his own, watching her as he takes a slow, careful sip. "Do you think I'm not in the thick of things?" he asks.

She gives a shrug, keeps looking at him. She sees him now as he had looked that day at Dartmoor's shooting range: When she turned away from Hurst he kept leaning against the car and staring at her, his head thrown back, his lips apart, teeth bared. Behind her, somewhere, was Hurst and the pathetic group of soldiers rehearsing their own demise, and she was among them, in an in-between world, a no-man's-land, and Jacobs stood there gaping, his eyes slits, inquisitive, stunned – no, he stood there all charged up – trying to peer into her world, like a schoolboy peeking into a tent full of women.

He looks at her a while with studied earnestness, his lips drawn over his teeth. "But in answer to your question, asthma," he said. "As simple as that. Unsuited to the trenches, but in my own way still good enough for my king."

She looks down at her glass, brings it to her lips, tastes the warm bitter beer. He is young, she thinks, not really my equal, still a child.

"And you?" There is nothing challenging in his gaze. "Why are you here?"

She considers the stock response for a moment, but then knows that this occasion, this place, does not warrant stock responses. That is not why she has come here. She recalls the tingling she felt earlier when sliding in next to him, the feeling that this proximity, its suddenness, might allow something totally unforeseen to occur. Whatever happens, she wants to confront it fearlessly, she wants to challenge it, she wants to be plunged into the melee. For a moment she considers the church bell dangling down into the icy depths of Crazywell, and then comes the ill-considered answer: "Because I wasn't really in the thick of things, not deep enough," she says.

It's as if her answer frightens her; she gives Jacobs a quick look. Nodding slowly, he seems to be thinking. "You mean in the Netherlands?" he says.

She shakes her head. "I'm not Dutch," she says. "I just work in the Netherlands." Now she must finish what she started. "I come from South Africa."

"I know," he says, and he must have noticed her surprise, as he then explains, "Sister Maxwell told me."

"Her!" She looks around at the women's table, but one of them is now talking and everyone is listening attentively. "I didn't think …" Why shouldn't she repeat the information?

"Surely it's not a secret?"

"No, it's not. It's just that it hasn't yet been mentioned."

"I did wonder about your reaction, that first time I fetched you, concerning that Rundle house."

"Oh, yes, I know. Sorry. It was silly of me."

"It did make sense to me, though, when I heard that you came from South Africa."

"Working as an orderly in a military hospital doesn't make you a psychologist."

166

"But it doesn't make me stupid either."

"The fact that you have a few pumpkin pips in your head does not give you the right to rummage around in other people's lives."

"Of course not," he says with a grimace, and turns around to call the barman.

She is left standing somewhat isolated, alone in a room full of people. The conversation has brought something to the fore that she couldn't foresee. Or perhaps it was inevitable, she's not sure, and she remains confused. She can also not rid herself of the feeling that she's experiencing some form of déjà vu, and now that her attention is no longer divided, it hits her: it's a childhood memory, in point of fact. It's actually something that often wells up in her, and she's tried countless times to analyse what she associates with it. It is a camp scene. Winburg. About to leave, she opens the tent flap, and bumps into Jannie de Villiers, the teenage soldier who was sent back from commando. He is caught red-handed, it's as clear as daylight. He was trying to peer in. He staggers back. "What are you up to in there?" he asks challengingly, accusingly, though with no apparent control over his facial expression.

"You're ... you're all naked in there." His voice breaks, he tries to convey his disgust with an exaggerated laugh, but it turns into a nervous giggle. There are bits of porridge between his teeth, a downy beard from his ears to his upper lip and chin, and both hands keep opening and closing. She sees the deep grooves in his thin, calloused fingers, filled with black grit. He's regained control over his facial muscles and looks at her expectantly, almost anxiously, his chest heaving below his tattered coat. Only once before had she seen him so upset, the time she and Alice asked whether he had seen the lancers. "Did you see them, Jannie, did you?" And he looked as if he had seen a ghost and he spoke about the huge horses with their trimmed tails, horses that ran like cats, leaping rather than running, and the long shiny spears the soldiers placed on the saddle between their hips, sitting straight up in full gallop, and how those long shiny blades are slowly lowered.

She feels the tap on her shoulder and turns around. Jacobs raises his glass to propose a toast, and she remembers the beer in her hands. She takes another sip. Jacobs holds his head to the side, looking down his nose at her, grinning, his upper lip pulled away from his teeth like a lusty ram. Susan looks at the froth on her beer, lifts the glass in greeting, turns around and walks back to the table where the women sit like four fingers of a fallen soldier that are sticking out of the sand. They're staring at her as if she were carrying something extraordinarily peculiar towards them, a new type of butterfly, a pixie she'd brought from Dartmoor, the head of John the Baptist on a platter. Under their enquiring gaze she sits down, pushing the beerglass towards the middle of the table with her fingertips, fixing her gaze on Anne's steady, mischievous eyes, her dear, dear eyes, and says: "Do it again."

"What?" Anne asks, but without the slightest indication that she is at all surprised at the request.

"Convulsions, fish flapping ..." A laugh erupts from behind her teeth. "And that spastic walk, the rolling eyes ..." She looks from one face to the next, scorching them with the fire that burned within her. "Give me the whole caboodle," she says in a fit of laughter that makes her bend forward and fall back again into the chair. "Give me the whole caboodle!"

Chapter 24

It's like when my eyes are shut tight, that's how dark it is in the train. At times I imagine that I'm seeing the white of a nurse's uniform across from me; the other one is sitting next to me, in the farthest corner. Are they still sitting up? I must have fallen asleep, and now it seems as if the train journey is only happening in my imagination, as if everyone sitting here is in my head. At times there are dark shadows at the window, like empty sacks blown in by the night. And sometimes a small fire that shoots sparks. Once, I heard someone call from outside, next to the track, and the sound was like a leaf torn from a tree by the wind, one moment it was there, and almost immediately it was far away and then gone.

Where could we be? I know that we have left Bloemfontein and we are on our way to the Cape, but there's just this great dark emptiness coming in through the windows and making it so dark inside that I can't see a thing. That's all there is. What that is, I am trying to remember. Jack Perry had stood next to the entrance saying he was just next door. The nurses spoke to each other in their own language. One of them asked my name, and when I told her, she said: Good, good and nodded her head and said her name was Betty and the other one's name was Clara. Luckily they did not say more than that, and I looked away and so I do not know what they were thinking.

I did not even put away the note that Dr Molesworth had given me. I also don't have to look at it, because I know all the words by heart. My name is written there. Miss S. Draper.

That is who I am now. Yesterday, when was it, three months ago, I was still someone else. Then something happened and now I am Susan Draper. No longer Nell. Susan Nell died in the camp. Along with Alice. I am certain Alice is also dead. But if I think about it, it's in a way she who is sitting in this train, I know so little of where I am or where I am going that it might just as well be she sitting here in this darkness.

All I am certain of is that I was in the camp at Winburg and then in the cave with Tiisetso and Mamello. Something happened, and now I am here on this train. I do actually know what happened, but I can't think about it now, it must first get light.

On the letter appear the words: *Upon presentation the following to be supplied to the bearer.* Then my name. My new name. *Miss S. Draper.* Then the medicine: *Two fluid oz. Quinine and 48 Cough Lozenges.* Then the doctor's name below: *Theodore Molesworth.* With MD after his name.

That is also the name that I gave to this nurse – Susan Draper. What is your name, she asked. Just like that, almost rude, but it's because they don't speak English well. Mostly, they speak to each other in their own language. That is also what I told the doctor. Earlier, when our coach stopped for the first time, in Bloemfontein – was that really yesterday? –

171

in front of a stone building with a low wall that had small turrets on either side, the doctor held an arm out towards me, just before he got out, and said: "Young lady, remind me of your name?" I got a fright, but he put his hand so gently on my arm, and I looked at his fingers, with the little hairs on them, and I waited for the hand to snap shut like a trap, but the doctor just continued quite normally. "With your surname," he said. "Then I'll give you a prescription that you can take to the pharmacy to get medicine for that throat of yours. All right?"

Then I said my name. Not very well, and I almost said Nell, and the doctor looked at me with tired eyes. He took a notebook and pencil from an inside pocket and wrote the prescription.

Afterwards it was just Perry and me in the coach. Jack was his name. The coach started moving again and he asked me where I was going. My mind froze, I couldn't say Bloemfontein, we were already in Bloemfontein, but where, where to? Where does one go in that place with its buildings like castles and streets full of carriages and women in immaculate dresses walking with parasols and its soldiers and horses? It's not like Winburg. Nor Heilbron either. I can even recall something of Ermelo, but in Bloemfontein it seems as if all the sounds, even the rattling of our coach and the hoofbeats and everything people say inside it, just stays like that in the street as if the buildings block everything and nothing can escape and everything will remain just as it is for ever and ever.

I knew that Perry was watching me and waiting for me

to respond, but I kept staring out of the window. When the coach stopped, he said: "Excuse me, but I quickly want to fetch something. I won't be long." Only then did I look at him again, but now he had his back to me and was opening the door.

Just before it closed I saw his face in the bright light, and I was alone in the coach with carts passing by and voices and every now and then the coach shook slightly when one of the horses moved. I could hear Perry talking to the coachman, and I sat and waited as I had in the cave in Winburg, but now with the fear that had climbed into the coach with me in front of the hotel in Winburg, the fear was like a porcupine that darted in under of my dress. But I just sat there, what else could I do?

He wasn't gone for long, and when he got back in he pressed a parcel into my hands. "You can't go to the Cape wearing that bonnet," he said. "You may as well be walking around with a Vierkleur in your hand – the Transvaal flag is like a red rag to a bull down there."

I took the package and as I opened it, I knew. I think that's the moment I began to trust him.

It was the hat – actually a type of cap – that I now have on my head. It is beautifully crocheted with blue-grey wool and it has a crochet flower above the ear and you can also pull the hat down low over your forehead. I'd seen the Englishwomen in Winburg wear it like that.

The coach began to move, and it wasn't long before it stopped again. "We're at the station," Perry said and opened the door. Lowering the lumpy bag at his feet to the ground, he climbed down. He turned to me and his glasses glinted in the sun. He held out a hand as if he wanted to help me off, but I pressed my pillowslip against my chest and climbed down by myself.

From the roof of the coach the Scout handed him two suitcases and a long slim leather bag. That was the first time I saw the Scout's face. Him I could easily look at, and he turned and glanced down at me; and I looked up, his head with the big hat was like a black sun in the blue sky, and I don't know why I saw it then, but there in front of me, right in front of me, so close that I could hear the horses huff, was a group of Bergh's Scouts on their horses with guns. The horses were packed so close together that they looked like a lump of shiny clay with their guns like porcupine quills stuck into it, and they came closer and it was as if those Scouts were laughing with one enormous, terrible mouth.

I see it again here in the night, that bunch of Scouts. It must have been something that flashed through my mind, because Perry then spoke and I had to look away from the barbarian who was unloading the things from the coach. "You'd better stay with me," and then he said, "We must make sure we board the train with the other women, because I can't travel alone with a woman."

I followed him because he didn't say this in a vulgar way. His luggage was being pushed along by a porter. And in a way I found it beautiful, those Scouts on the horses and how they galloped by, so close to one other, full speed across the veld, through the tents, through Winburg, and how the horses' hooves hammered everything, everything, everything into

174

dust so that nothing remained behind, nothing, nothing, nothing.

Inside the station a whole lot of people were pushing and shoving like in the food queues at the camp, but now there were also Khakis in the commotion – I'd got used to them in the camp – and people in beautiful clothes and blacks carrying bags or pushing them on carts, but then I saw it for the very first time.

It was suddenly just there, and the noise made me put my hands to my ears, iron and steam and the light flashing on a copper ball and a man with a big belly standing at the door with his jacket flapping open like a tent and then the wagons full of burghers jammed together with their grubby gaunt faces singing "Prijs den Heer".

Perry must have seen me get a fright, because he came to stand next to me. "Prisoners of war," he said. And then he and I stood watching the departing train, one wagon after the next filled with bedraggled burghers praising the Lord. Why? Why praise the Lord with all your soul? Is it not better to be dead than to have stood there on that cement with ants racing around in circles and stones that crunch under my hot shoes or being there in those stinking wagons that are taking them ... where? Where are they taking them?

Perry leaves me at the baggage cart, and I watch him trying to make his way through the throng. My shoes are too big. The sleeves of my dress are too long. From afar, the men's singing still reverberates. Like when we used to sing in the camp and it sounded to me as if the hymn made the tent puff up like a hen, that's how the burghers sang on that crowded station with its noise and its smell like a red-hot horseshoe. That's how they sang, with the people on the platform seemingly held back by a huge hand that only released them once the train had disappeared into the heat of the day and when I could no longer hear the voices, only then did the people step forward once again.

Then Perry was suddenly with me again; I hadn't seen him coming at all. He held tickets in his hand and said: "So, Miss Draper, from now on you're an employee of Jack Perry's Photographic Services in Cape Town." That is how Jack Perry spoke. "I have your ticket; I'll keep it with me until we board." What could I say? In any case my English was not good enough.

I just stood there awkwardly with my head half-hidden beneath the new hat. Perhaps I said something, I don't know any more, but Perry kept talking and said he needed someone like me who could help him with his cameras and assist when he had to take portraits at people's homes or anywhere else.

Someone like me? What does he mean by that? Here I am, sitting in a dark train in the night and I have nothing and no one. Everyone is dead, and I am not even sure that I am alive. Pa is dead. Ma. Neelsie. Alice. Perhaps I'm on my way to the place where the dead go. To heaven. But it's too dark for that, I think.

Perry wanted to take a photograph of a group of soldiers who were standing around on the platform. Most of them were in bandages, or leaning on crutches. The wounded. He then asked them to pose, and they laughed and chatted, and

Perry took a camera from that lumpy bag and gave it to me. While he was preparing to take the picture another train came in, wheels screeching on the tracks, the wagons filled with wood and corrugated iron and blacks in blankets on top who are just staring out at all the people. I looked back at the soldiers who were posing for their portrait, and one of them whose helmet strap was cutting into his cheek looked at me, his lips curled back like a ruttish ram.

I looked at him and felt something inside me filling up slowly, slowly, like when you fill a basin with water, and I know that I'll be thrown out with the dirty water, that I am bad and sinful and that I do not even deserve to be on a train, and shouldn't be going anywhere at all.

I don't know what happened then, but Perry looked round at me with a worried expression on his face and then he took the camera from me and squatted next to the bag to pack the things away again.

I now know what I'd seen. The gold buttons of the wounded soldier who looked at me like that. The buttons on his uniform. Some kind of design engraved on them. The shiny gold buttons. It was in a tent. The button had broken loose and spun around once on the groundsheet and then it lay there. And another man had picked it up.

It was Uncle Krisjan Schutte who'd picked up the button. Now I know. It was also him on the farm. He's the one who'd hitched up his trousers with both hands as if he were picking up a sack. When Ma and I … when Ma was still alive. It was him.

It's like travelling inside your own head, a train in the night

177

like this. A war train that may not cast any light, otherwise the Boers will see it and shoot. I must not think. Only when it gets light, yes. Only then.

Chapter 25

The room is filled with bright light! Alarmed, she sits up and throws the blankets off. She's completely overslept; why did Mrs Simms not wake her, the hospital transport would have left long ago. She grabs some clothing, pulls the door open and dashes to the bathroom. Somewhere, Mrs Simms is busying herself; she hears soft humming and a cupboard door slam shut. Carefully she pushes the door closed and stands with her back to it, breathing deeply, trying to gather her thoughts. The Sphinx. Four or five of them, zig-zagging home, arm in arm; she'd said her goodbyes on the corner so that she could enter the house quietly. Her head only allows her that, the memory of the walk back through the night, Anne's fingers fleetingly in hers, the warm, slightly clammy hand that slid from her own.

She pushes herself away from the door, pours water into the washbasin and lets her nightdress fall from her shoulders. Taking a cloth, she begins to wash her throat and her shoulders, and the mirror in front of her reflects a face full of shadows, the curve of her shoulder, the hollow at her collarbone. She tries to remember something of last night's dream, but it eludes her, only a vague unease remains, a dim outline that hovers just out of sight. She wipes the cold rough cloth over her breasts and their sensitive nipples, cups her hands below their soft weight, the cloth hanging from one hand, then she imagines someone else's hands, and she closes her eyes against her reflection so that she doesn't have to see any of this.

Mrs Simms called out from behind the door. The motorbike man, she said. Susan quickly got dressed. Could it really be Jacobs? She greeted Mrs Simms with an apologetic laugh, and this time the old woman's condescension was appropriate, even comforting.

Jacobs is already astride the bike, his lips curve in greeting like those of a fish, tapering to a point, his nose is tilted upwards as he hands her the goggles on the seat of the sidecar. He pulls his goggles over his eyes, and without looking at her he grumbles, "You should thank Sister Maxwell."

Once she is seated, Jacobs hits the gearshift on the tank between his legs and the bike leaps forward. They thunder down the street, hardly stopping at the corner and she's forced to cling on as the sidecar's wheel almost lifts up. The roar is left hanging among the houses in the empty street and they are plucked from the town towards what looks to her like a farm road, between lanes, meadows and fields, the low stone walls drooping in moss. The wind presses her uniform against her body, tugging at her hair. She sees how the ends of Jacobs's jacket flap against his thighs, their thick bulge. She sees his determination and focused concentration as he guides the bike onto the smoothest parts of the road. She is strangely moved, utterly transported. He is a man, a soldier. She is carried away by the speed, the landscape flashing past, the almost reckless vitality, the life force, the fearless thundering forward that makes the frightened trees give way.

Yes, she thinks, yes!

And suddenly it is over. She gets out, takes the goggles off. Smoothes her hair. Shakes it loose. Her whole body is tingling, the shuddering of the engine still inside her, the joy of light and wind and flickering leaves still in her breath. She walks over the gravel to the archway, crosses the courtyard, walks in the mild sun with the echo of her footsteps. Life can triumph, she now knows, and she also knows what she needs to do.

She fetches Hamilton-Peake's folder from where it lies hidden in her drawer in the service room and goes looking for Hurst. Once again, he watches her almost warily as she walks towards his desk and sits down. She crosses her legs, sees how his eyes dart to her knees for a fraction of a second, and flick up again. He sits back in his chair. She uncrosses her legs, keeps the file flat on her lap, takes a deep breath before speaking. He tilts his head in anticipation.

She clears her throat. "I've been thinking," she says, "we should take the patient in room 114 for a motorbike ride." She realises that she still cannot say his name, and the realisation makes her lose heart.

"You're not serious?" Hurst says, though his mouth settles into a bemused smile, his eyes gleaming like water in dark pools. She does not answer him, knowing that her eyes, her face, her proud bearing, will have to convince him. And then he says: "Will Jacobs be able to manage this?"

"No, not him," she says, and exhales softly, quietly.

"Who, then, one of the other orderlies?"

"No," she says, her eyes cast down, then she looks him straight in the eye. "No, I'll drive."

"You!"

"I'll just drive a little way down the road and then back again. In the Netherlands I had a friend who had a motorbike and he let me drive sometimes."

Hurst sits watching her for a while. Why? he's supposed to ask, but he doesn't, he doesn't. Their eyes are fixed on each other, and she tries to sustain the brute yammering of the machine deep inside her; she lets her face, her whole body say it: This is real life! Then he throws his hands in the air. He must realise there is no turning back. He should have said no from the outset, but now it's too late.

Jacobs brings the motorbike to the front gate. Susan puts her hands on the steering wheel and waits. Helmet on, goggles over her eyes. The trio comes hobbling through the gate. Between Hurst and Jacobs is the patient from room 114. Colonel Hamilton-Peake. The two men support him as his head lolls and his legs swing under a calf-length dressing gown.

Susan tries to kick-start the bike. Her shoe slips, and she does not succeed. She laughs nervously, and Jacobs comes to help. She gets off, lets him get the bike going. She watches him carefully, is aware of Hurst loading the patient into the sidecar.

Jacobs tries to put a helmet on his head, but Susan stops him. "I want him to feel the wind," she says, "the freedom, the outdoors." She throws her arms wide and laughs, but knows that her face is in fact painfully contorted, as if she wants to cry, because she's almost overwhelmed by the realisation that she is standing on the threshold between darkness and light, that she is on a motorbike, at the verge of breaking through the thin membrane separating life and death.

Jacobs looks at Hurst. Hurst nods thoughtfully.

Susan pushes the accelerator, the bike sputters. "Here we go!" she shouts as she hits the gear lever in front of her to the right and lets go of the clutch. The bike lurches forward.

"Slowly!" Jacobs calls from behind, and she glances over her shoulder. Sees the two men with their hands by their sides staring at her, and some people leaning out of windows. The wheels crunching over gravel, the juddering roar, earth shooting by below them. Hamilton-Peake clinging on, his face contorted in fear, horror. The shrubs parting in front of them, the bending trees, the smell of wheat and sunlight and petrol fumes. What on earth am I doing? she thinks, suddenly panicky. What's got into me? Then she pulls the clutch, slaps the bike into a higher gear and accelerates. She feels the power of the engine, the vibration against her thighs, the wind tugging at her clothes. Yes, that's it, that is all that matters, this feeling that we are alive. She thinks of her hands pushed in under Jacques's jacket, just the thin cotton of his shirt between her fingers and the skin over his ribs. She begins to laugh, a chuckle rattles from her mouth, a low throaty sound that rises and rises with the roar of the engine into the screech of some kind of bird of prey, she thinks. It's as if she can hear herself from a distance, as if she has left her body, and is hovering just above the motorbike, through the warm morning redolent of

183

deep soil and seed and horse sweat and the moistness of skin rubbing against skin and two bodies utterly surrendered to nothing, nothing, nothing.

She charges up a hill and the landscape unfolds in front of them. She releases the accelerator and, half-dazed, she starts braking, takes the bike out of gear and lets it rumble along until she hears the light crunch of the wheels as it comes to a halt.

She's panting, as if she'd been running. They sit, surrounded by the low sputtering of the engine, the sticky air, the day that spills so green, so verdant between golden fields of wheat.

For a long while they sit like that. She does not look at him. Does not hear him, does not see him, just knows that he is there. Not even when she starts speaking does she look at him. "Perhaps you remember," she says. But then she fails to say what she wanted to say.

She lets go of the accelerator carefully, making sure that the engine does not stall. Then she takes both hands off the handlebars, removes the goggles and helmet and gives her head a shake. She climbs off the motorbike and walks up to the sidecar.

Hamilton-Peake's right hand lies limp on its rim. His head is still tilted in a spasm, his eyes searchlights swinging across the cloudless sky. She bends down, takes his cold hand and brings it to her face, presses the fingertips against her forehead, presses them to her scalp, allows them to find the ridge of the scar, gently wriggles his fingers – over the little spine that lies there in a lovely arc, vertebra for vertebra, nerve for nerve.

Was there perhaps something? Was there some movement in his fingers, in his eyes, in the angle of his head, the tension of his neck muscles ... was there any sign that he felt something?

She rides back slowly, almost at a crawling pace in first gear, and her thoughts drift away from him to herself. What did it mean for her? What did she feel? But her thoughts congeal, becoming a thick and unmanageable mass, and all she can really register is the vibration in her palms, in her arms, in her back and behind, down to her toes. Her teeth are rattling a bit. She jiggles her head as if bothered by a bee, as if she wants to shake something off, but she can't rid herself of the realisation that it's not just the bike's vibrations that are making her shake so uncontrollably. She was wrong, she'd made a terrible mistake. She had allowed herself to be misled. This here is not life, no, no, no, this is death. This convulsive skeleton next to her, he came to her in the guise of the sun and the wind, the fertile earth, and she could not see that it was only a mask, because at any moment this monster was going to rip it off and force my legs open with his knee and ram his thing into me.

Her elbows held tight against her body, she rides into the hospital grounds. Hurst and Jacobs are still in front of the building, pacing about, their necks straining to see where and when they'd arrive. She rides directly towards them. Right up to them.

The trembling is in her arms. She feels the rhythm of a cantering horse, the kick of huge muscles between her legs, the heaving of enormous lungs. She feels the weight of the

185

long lance couched on her arm, she holds it in her hand and prods the horse; she sees the one man cowering against an anthill, frozen with fear, she lowers the lance, the horse gives one last cat-like leap, and with the full momentum of rider and horse she allows the lance to slip from her hip and slide through cotton-skin-blood, through organs, through the compacted soil, and when she brings the motorbike to rest in front of Hurst and Jacobs, her consciousness is still filled with the wild teeming of a mass of white termites on the blood-smeared tip of a lance.

With shaking hands she rips off the goggles and helmet, and as her feet touch the ground she turns her back to the two anxious, staring men, bending forward and smoothing her lap, concerned that traces of what had just taken place would be visible on her face and clothes.

Chapter 26

Dawn. The relentless clack-clacking of the train. Barbed wire. Blockhouses. The nurse called Betty had pulled her feet in and lay with her head on a round blue pillow covered in the same smooth leather as the seating on the train. Inside, it's all wood, almost to the ceiling. The ceiling is painted white. Between the two benches is a door with a shiny metal latch; that's how you get into the corridor, and Perry showed me where to go when nature called.

The nurse is awake now and brushing her long white hair. She smiled and said good morning when she saw me staring at the brush swishing with long smooth strokes through her hair, and at her face turning away from the whishing brush, her mouth pulled down, but it was a skew smile that made me feel that I could look.

With her chin, the nurse gestures at the window, and I see a blockhouse flash past with a Khaki in front looking as if he has just gone outside. "Soldiers," said the nurse, "do you like them?"

I keep looking out of the window, not at the blockhouse, but at the empty veld. She laughs, and I hear the swishing sound of her brush. The other nurse has also woken up; she's come to stand by the window and she opens it, sticks her chest out and waves. Something is bumping against the compartment, behind the seats, I can feel the vibration at my back. And there are voices too. Soldiers' voices.

I look at Betty. "No," I say, "I don't like them."

"I know," she says, "you're not one of them." I look down at Dr Molesworth's note in my hand.

"You're a Boer," says Betty.

Clara pulls back from the window, turns around. Betty pins her hair up. "It's not important," says Clara. "Don't be afraid." She sits next to me. "We like the Boers too."

"Do you know De Wet?" Betty asks. "Have you seen him?" She looks at Clara and they both begin to laugh.

When they've stopped laughing Betty says to me: "We have seen him, in Thaba Nchu. He walks like this," and she makes snaking movements with her hand, and starts laughing again.

"He walks fast," Clara says between snorts. "He doesn't stop, not that one."

Why are they telling me this? I know that they mean something other than what they are saying, and I think I know what this is. I don't like it when people act as if I know nothing …

Alice sometimes did this, like the time Jannie de Villiers told us about the English at Ladysmith who'd stuffed the barrel of the Long Tom full of gunpowder. The burghers then took the broken cannon back to Pretoria, where they simply sawed off a section of the barrel so that it could shoot again. After this, the burghers no longer called the cannon Long Tom, but The Jew. Alice laughed and laughed and laughed, Jannie too, and they looked at me and made hand gestures indicating that I was stupid.

Alice often asked me if I liked Jannie de Villiers, and when I said no, she'd say, but he likes you. Sometimes we followed him around, hanging onto each other and shouting after him. "Jan!" she'd shout, and then I shouted "Makapan!" When he got angry we said to him: "Oh, Jannie, we just want to hear about the war."

Then he said: "What do you girls know?"

Jannie ran away from home to join the commando, but he was sent back because he was too young. One day he just arrived at the camp on a foal – his feet almost touching the ground. The horse came walking slowly between the tents with Jannie clinging to its mane. Then his mother recognised him and helped him off and into the tent. One of the turncoats came to take his gun away, and gave it to the camp guards.

"How many Khakis did you shoot?" I yelled.

"Do you shoot them here, Jannie, here?" Alice shouted with a little leap, her bum facing him with her finger pressed to it. We laughed, Alice and I, we laughed and laughed.

Jannie had tied his father's pocket watch to his wrist with leather strips. He says when you are fighting, you can't be struggling with a watch chain hooking onto everything, or a watch that falls out when the lyddite bombs start going off and you need to dive among some rocks.

"But it's your father's watch, Jannie, not yours!" we said.

Then Jannie says nothing. We don't know what happened to his father, or to his brother. But Jannie did once say: "If my brother comes back he'll come and get the two of you."

Someone knocks on the door, and when Clara enquires who it is, Perry answers.

As the door opens he immediately looks at me, and then at the two nurses. He gives a little smile and enquires after my health. I nod. "We could have breakfast at Beaufort West," he says. Then I say I want to leave for a minute and he slides the door open for me.

There is no one else in the corridor, and I don't in fact want to go to the lavatory. I didn't want to look outside either; I knew the sun was there and the veld and the barbed wire and the blockhouses with soldiers looking at the disappearing train. I thought about Krisjan Schutte coming to take Jannie's gun, hitching his trousers before he bent down into the tent. And I thought of the night he bent low to the tarpaulin, slap-slapping after the gold button rolling away.

Perry slid the door shut and came to stand next to me. "Where are you from?" he asked.

I did not look at him. "You know," I said. "Winburg."

"From the camp?"

I looked at him. I looked him straight in the eye, but I said nothing.

"Here's Beaufort West," he said. "Not too long now, and we'll be in the Cape."

Chapter 27

Mrs Simms mentions that a letter has arrived for her, and she quickly walks to her room. At the foot of her bed, on the folded bedspread, lies a letter with the red one-penny stamp of the Union of South Africa showing the profile of a heavily moustached King George in an oval frame.

It looks a bit like Jack, she thinks, and strokes the stamp with a fingertip that strays to the address written in the compact yet flowing hand of her only remaining contact with her fatherland. The irony had not struck her before, the similarity between Jack Perry and the British king. The letter had been forwarded from an office in Dordrecht, she notices, and tears open the envelope.

Jack tells her that he'd thought about her again when he met a woman with the surname Draper. She'd walked into his shop to make an appointment for a photographic session. An elegant woman from Simon's Town. Jack asked whether she knew an Alice Draper who had been in the concentration camp in Winburg, but the woman said no and then became quite curt. He doubts now that she'll arrive for the appointment. No more on the topic. Further to that, he writes that the country is in the destructive grip of the worldwide flu and that on a farm between Cape Town and Stellenbosch eighteen children were buried on one day.

She scrunches the paper between her fingers. She tries to imagine something of what Jack has described. She has never been to Stellenbosch, she hears there's a university there now.

She tries to recall Cape Town, the station, Strand Street, the sea, but all she manages to visualise is herself in front of Jack Perry's camera, in front of the cold shiny eye of the lens.

She sits brooding with Jack Perry's letter in her hands. From her homeland, the place she comes from, that is the image that comes most clearly to mind, that makes all others fade into the background: her standing in front of that scrutinising eye, the eye that can no longer see the expansive land, the veld and the dust, the soaring pale blue sky and the red sun. The eye that can only look inwards at her heart and see her guilt, the complicity. She knows it, she also knows what it is, because she can also look at herself objectively and be analytical. Early on in the Netherlands, in Reymaker's clinic, but also during her training in the Meerenberg institution, she saw other women who had been ground under a heel, completely and utterly crushed, yet still could not free themselves from the thought that they were the snake, that they deserved it, that the poison had always been in them.

Even her rebirth after such a trampling, the triumph of leaving her motherland behind, soon dissipated, its original ecstasy waning. She remembers that she turned away from the shimmering sea and the mountain fading on the horizon and all that she could see was the ship's chimney that spat black smoke into the clear air and the cruel rigging and creaking steel cables. And something more, later on, also on the ship. In a cabin, not hers, but she was standing, and behind her a woman was sitting on a bed, and the woman looked at her and the woman hated her, loathed her, because the woman could see who and what she really was and what she was up to. How often it haunts her, that scene with its indescribable tension, which for her is also entirely understandable, even explicable, but at the same time utterly unfathomable.

She was one of forty-seven first class passengers on the *Glenart Castle*. Because she was travelling alone, she could have a single cabin. Small, dark, swaying … oppressive! After the captain – or was it one of the crew? – pulled the door shut behind her she began unpacking her clothes, but quickly snapped her suitcase shut and hurried out. She spent her days in the dining hall or on one of the decks, and in the evenings tried to fall asleep as quickly as possible.

Most of the passengers were English-speaking, but there was one Dutch couple, they were elderly. Mr and Mrs De Goede. They had been in the country long enough for her to be able to speak Afrikaans freely with them, although she only had the courage to do so after the woman gave her a spoonful of ground ginger for sea sickness. "Keep your eyes on the horizon whenever possible, my child," Mr de Goede moaned with a sigh that sounded like breath being blown through his mouth with a bellows.

She soon realised that, often, he would sit and watch her, that Mr De Goede. His eyes darted like lizards beneath his bushy eyebrows, and his long upper lip was a tortoise-like beak. After a couple of days at sea she began to itch terribly, and he of course noticed. "It's nothing other than lice, my child," he said from across the table. "This ship is, after all, used for soldiers." He straightened up in his chair, his eyes flicked to his wife, and then he said: "Come. Come with us to our cabin. I have something that will help."

It feels as if that scene is being replayed inside her, as if her entire inner self is being wrung like soapy water from a sheet. That moment when she almost froze in terror and turned her bewildered gaze at Mrs De Goede, she relives as acutely as if she were back in the ship's dining room.

Mrs De Goede had simply picked up her bag and started walking. In the cabin she sat on a bunk, bag on her lap, bolt upright, like a dog begging for a bit of fat. Mr De Goede pulled a suitcase from under his bed, similar to the one Dr Molesworth had. He opened it and began to unpack things onto the table next to the bunk: a pestle, mortar, small spoon and two tins. He opened a tin and spooned something into the mortar. "Ordinary tea leaves," he said. "Very finely ground." Only then did he look up at her where she had remained awkwardly standing in the middle of the cabin. "Come and sit down, my dear," he said, pointing to the bunk where his wife was seated and scratching the grey whiskers that ran from his shiny pate past his ears to below his jaw.

She sat down and saw him leaning over the mortar, cupping his left hand over his mouth and spitting loudly into the receptacle.

With his right hand he took a handkerchief from his

pocket, and as he was about to wipe his mouth she glimpsed a thread of spit hanging between his lips and the mortar. She shuddered, intensely aware of the dour, silent woman next to her.

"Please excuse this," Mr De Goede wheezed, "it's unfortunately the only way, water won't work." He opened the other tin and very carefully stirred about with the spoon. "Mercury," he said, his mouth so close to the tin that his voice had a dull echo. With a lightly trembling hand he held a quivering bright droplet in a spoon and let it slide into the mortar. Mr De Goede went to work with the pestle, his eyebrows jumping around like two fighting skunks as he concentrated on the grinding, which made a sound like chattering teeth.

Susan looked at Mrs De Goede again, noticing that her head was tilted, her lips parted, like a mother watching a child trying to tie a shoelace for the first time. The older woman was swallowing with some difficulty.

The old greybeard took a piece of thick string from his suitcase; he lowered one end into the mortar and used the pestle to blend it with the mixture. Every now and then he looked at Susan, and when he was satisfied with whatever was happening in the bowl, he lifted his left hand and held it out to Susan. "Come a bit closer, my dear," he said, exhaling above the dome of his stomach.

She had stood up carefully, stepped closer, and taken one more cautious step until she was just in front of him. She saw the string in the mortar, like a small brown snake.

Using the fingers of one hand, Mr De Goede took hold of both ends of the string and lifted it out, allowing it to fall in a loop. He beckoned her with his left hand. "Come closer, my dear, if you'd just bend forward a little, then …" His fingers lured her, closer and closer.

She looked around quickly at the woman behind her. Saw her hands clutching the top of her bag, her face worried. And then she felt Mr De Goede's fingers around her neck, and she staggered back.

He stood there, both hands in the air, with one in the loop, as if he were trying to lasso a wild horse. Reassuringly, he closed his eyes and gave a light shake of his head. "If you'd just pull your collar away a little, I could tie the string around your neck," he said. "You wear it where no one can see it, and that's the end of the lice. You'll see."

She slowly bent down, and he fastened the string as if it were a necklace. He pushed his hands under her hair, his head was so close that she could feel the warmth of his body, she could see the pores and the strands of grey hair on his scalp. Then his hands slid down her shoulders and he straightened her collar, his eyes probing her face in concern. She shut her eyes tight, felt him brush her hair from her face and his warm dry fingertips crawl up her forehead to where she knew he could now see the scar. Mrs De Goede's eyes burned into her back, she wanted to pull away and run, but she was completely immobile, trapped between the man's probing fingers and the woman's searing gaze. They know, she'd thought to herself, they know.

She leaps up from the bed, unable to pursue the memory any further; Perry's crumpled letter is still in her hands. Yet again, she tries to free herself from the woman's scrutiny –

the judge-mental, damning gaze of the woman who sits and watches her husband as well as Susan. She feels herself shrivel, sinks down onto the bed, smoothes the pages of the letter and starts reading again, feverishly trying to find something, anything, to banish those memories from this room with its mute walls, its silent curtains, its heartless furniture.

Gradually she regains her hold on what Jack has written, slowly new images arise in her mind. Who was the Draper woman in Jack's shop? It's as if there are shadows moving behind a curtain. Alice had relatives in Simon's Town, she sometimes spoke about them, but her father's people came from Ladybrand. From deep soil and green vegetation and smooth, round rocks and poplars that shiver in the wind. She tries to recall the land Jack writes about – her land – but her thoughts become entangled again, this time in something she cannot place, though not for want of trying. A bizarre image. All she knows is that it has something to do with what happened earlier that day at the hospital, but it's also as if the image has always been there, from the beginning, without her being aware of it. It's as if everything that is flooding her thoughts has always been present.

It's a dance scene. She and Alice and Hamilton-Peake dancing among the tents at Winburg camp, they are dancing in a fine cloud of golden dust, arms locked, a closed circle, spinning wildly like a whirlwind, around and around, his hand warm and dry against her arm, the fabric of his uniform softer than she'd imagined – oh, but you are *monate*, he says, you are delicious, and she wants to adjust her dress that has slipped from her shoulders again, but she can't break

197

the circle of hands, and Alice is also looking at her, laughing with her mouth wide open and her head thrown back, and she feels their hands grow cold on her skin, and she sees their eyes freeze, how they die in her arms, and she remains standing, the only one – the only one who is still alive in this godforsaken country, the only one who is still alive.

She had to leave that country, life itself made certain of that, but to keep what alive? That was my beginning and my end, she thought. My beginning and my end.

She will write to Perry tonight. She will write about the hospital and her work, about the country and its people. About Jacobs and Anne and Hurst. Yes, about Hurst too, but what? She likes him, he is definitely very clever, but for some reason their interaction always turns into something that it shouldn't really be. And it was like that long before she knew about Hamilton-Peake. Oh, she doesn't know any more, she hates being at the mercy of things inside her that she can't get a proper grip on.

There's a cutting from *The Times* that she wants to include in her letter. It was the ship's name that led her eye to the article. The *Glenart Castle*. She'd left the Cape on that ship, and now it is a watery grave. Torpedoed on 26 February. The ship's matron, Katy Beaufoy, was among the casualties. Susan remembered how her heart had trembled when she heard that Katy had also been in the Anglo-Boer War. She was the matron at the military hospital in Exeter when the war broke out. She volunteered, and was in South Africa for the duration of the war. Her first journey on the *Glenart Castle* was also her last.

Sometimes, she muses to herself – it's the first time Susan has had this thought since that dark journey from the concentration camp – sometimes it is better when a journey ends early.

Chapter 28

The train jerks and slows down again. Are we there yet? Is this the end of the road? Perhaps it's just another station, another town. Trees move past, drab trees baking in the sun. There is a great big building like a castle. Perhaps we are in Cape Town.

Betty and Clara start collecting their things; they must have noticed my confusion, as Betty tells me that this is Matjiesfontein. This is where they get off. They're on their way to the military hospital.

Cape Town, that's where I'm going. To do what, precisely? What will become of me? It will be revealed to me, Mamello had said. I don't know whether she believes in God, that I don't know, but I suspect so.

I say goodbye to the nurses with a handshake. They laugh, and it makes me angry.

Through the window you can see that many people are getting off here. It's overrun with Tommies. All the wounded who boarded in Bloemfontein are leaving, it seems, but there's also a group in new, clean uniforms. Also a bunch of women in long pleated dresses and funny little flat hats and a few with parasols to shield themselves against the sun. They're speaking English. Betty and Clara are also walking there, and there are more nurses.

Soldiers and nurses. That's what this world is made up of. Those who wound, and those who have to heal the wounds.

I don't know how people like Jack Perry fit in there. He just watches. He stands behind his camera and looks at what's going on there in front. He's at enough of a distance so as not to become part of the war.

That's probably how the Lord does it too. He looks on from afar. And He turns His face away from that which does not please Him. Instead, He looks at this bare stony veld. Whose side is He on, on the side of those who die or those who kill? There are after all also Boers who kill. And die. They who die, who are buried in this soil, between the bushes, they go unto Him. The others, the guilty ones, who are rotting and contaminated from within, they ... Yes, what happens to them?

And as if the Lord Himself has heard me, I see them coming. The first time I saw them they were getting down from a carriage about three ahead of ours, the two soldiers, one with a gun slung over his shoulder and the other pushing something into the front pocket of his uniform. Tommies. They are walking alongside the train, and I don't know how, but suddenly I know what they're doing – they are checking people's passes!

All I can do is to sit and watch. I want to jump up, but I can't, my legs are too weak, my whole body seems to be like porridge that has spilt onto the seat. Now I know what is going to happen to me, the Lord has answered. And when

I see them getting onto the train, I see it, and when they're inside, I find the strength.

Luckily I don't have to struggle with the door, and just outside, in the corridor, stands Jack Perry. He turns around to look at me as he hears the door open. And I just stand there, looking at him, and cannot utter a word. I can't get a word out. Next to him, through the window, I can see the veld.

The hard dry veld full of stones and rising to a low hill, drab and bare and empty, with the sun that's somewhere, I don't know where, but the sun is above and within and part of everything – it in fact radiates outwards from the soil.

"Just go and sit down," Jack said. "And try not to be afraid. I'll talk to them."

I don't know how he became aware of them. He probably just saw my face and knew. They too will see my face and know. They will know.

All I can do now is wait. Look straight ahead and wait. Shut my eyes tight and wait. What will they do with me? I try to think, but I can't, I can't let my thoughts go there. All I can see is the empty veld, the warm stones, I feel the heat coming through the window, hear the rocks calling out, the echoing trumpets, and the footsteps down the hallway. They want to see the passes, the voices say. I was right, they were looking for me, this is the end. The end is like this veld where you can see nothing and everything. Everything is there, even if you cannot see it, even if you cannot see it, it is there. Like the sun.

I don't know how long I've been sitting here, but suddenly the train lurches. And again. Where is Jack Perry? The train moves forward. The buildings recede. The people. The soldiers. The soldiers.

What is the Lord's plan, then? It will be revealed to me, Mamello said. It will be revealed to me.

Chapter 29

Hurst is waiting in the passage when she arrives that morning, in the bright light falling through a window half his pale face is hidden by a shadow.

"Is something wrong?" she asks.

"Come and look," he says somewhat absently, then turns around and starts walking.

Long before they get there, she guesses their destination. Room 114.

Hurst stands with his hand on the doorknob and waits for her to catch up before he turns it. She is behind him, her head down, and she notices the kink in the hem of his trousers just above his field boots. The door clicks open, and as the hinge squeaks she wants to grab onto the door, prevent a disturbance.

She walks into the dim room behind the smooth back of Hurst's carefully ironed uniform.

Colonel Hamilton-Peake is lying under a sheet. It forms a little tent over his nose, and the white fabric seems to have been sucked in by a dying mouth taking its last breath.

Before she can stop herself, Susan swings around, almost into Hurst's chest. He takes a step backwards. His eyes rest on her a moment and then look over her shoulder, searching, no, inquisitive rather, as if he is surreptitiously trying to ferret out the cause of her upset.

What does he want to know? Why did he bring her here?

"Why did you do this?" she asks, startled by the hoarseness of her voice.

His eyes flash at her; a worried frown on his forehead, fingertips at his chest, his eyes darting between her and the bed.

"Why did you bring me here?"

He takes a step, turns sideways, seemingly to get the silent bed outside of his field of vision so as to give her his full attention. He could simply have informed her. After all, in the first instance, this is his patient. He's the one who wanted to get him healthy and back into the trenches. To go and fight for his damn king. She is almost blinded by fury. "You blame me, don't you?" She just manages to control her voice. "That's why you brought me here. You think I killed him."

He is still looking at her with a worried expression. "It was life or death," he says. "It could have gone either way. You were aware of this, weren't you?"

She looks away. What if he were sitting up in his bed? she thought. As lively as a cricket? If I'd saved his life?

Hurst addresses the side of her face: "Because you got involved, for the very reason that you became so intimately involved, I thought you'd have wanted to know – wanted to see." He folds his arms across his chest and his professional restraint gives way to an irritability she's never noticed in him before. "The way us doctors usually do," he says, glaring from under his eyebrows.

"Us doctors!" She spits out the words. "Suddenly I am one of 'us'. Obviously, now I get it – now that there's a corpse in the bed, I am suddenly one of the boys. Now I'm part of this whole sick game of …" She looks for the words, realises she can't see him properly, and slaps her hands against her sides. Hurst recoils in the face of her attack, and takes another step sideways. They start circling each other like boxers. Her eyes dig into his face, chipping away at the noble façade, the unblemished visage. Doctors! Like the one who'd sat in that cursed tent while the whole of Winburg was coughing and puking snot and guts and pain and misery, and without batting an eyelid he'd taken that gleaming, sparkling, fire-spitting pen of his and written, God knows, he'd written that the cause of my death, that the cause of my death, that the cause of my death …

She freezes. Mutely, she looks left and right, just not at the bed. The door is still ajar, behind it the dull white walls of the corridor. She stands gasping, her hand to her throat. Somewhere, the familiar hospital sounds. Someone calling, something falling. Footsteps. "That's what doctors do," she hears herself saying. And she looks at him again. Silently. And against her will her eyes slide down; against all reason, she gives in to her eyes' longing to slip into that impenetrable slit of his mouth to find something soft and loving there and also something utterly rebellious. "I'm sorry," she says, "I should have known."

Chapter 30

It's far bigger than the one in Bloemfontein, Cape Town's station. Far more people too, far more noise. And the people have far more beautiful clothes. Even the blacks are better dressed, but Perry tells me they're not the ones I am used to. I can see that, they're not as black, and they have smooth shiny hair, and they're very rude and they say improper things and then laugh loudly and crudely. And there I stand with Perry, in among all the people, and it's a bit uncomfortable for me, and also for Jack, I can see that. He peers over the people as if he were looking for something.

Most of the English soldiers got off at Matjiesfontein, at the hospital, but a few healthy ones also boarded there to eventually join a ship bound for England. As the train nears the station I glimpse the sea and my stomach gives a lurch. At first I don't know what I'm looking at and just keep staring at the flat shiny thing that is lying there. It doesn't occur to me that it's all water.

I don't know what we're going to do now. Jack says his house is somewhere in the city and that is where he lives with his wife. They don't have any children, and there's enough space for me to stay there for a while until something else comes up. That's what he told me when he came to sit with me in the compartment after Matjiesfontein. By then I was speaking to him easily, there was nothing more to hide. He knows who I am and where I come from, and he is not one of the enemy, even though he speaks English and works for the British. He understands me and can speak a few words of Afrikaans. We speak to each other without any difficulty.

Jack says he has a photography business in the city, but before the war he also had to sell furniture to make enough money. Now he works mainly for the imperial government, who pay well for photographs of the war. That's why he was in Winburg. He also spent long periods with the British columns in the veld, never at any of the pitched battles, he said, though he did witness a few minor skirmishes. That's what Jack told me as more and more mountains surrounded the train and I could no longer see blockhouses or barbed wire next to the tracks.

For a while Jack sat with me and watched the veld, which by then looked completely different to the Free State, and then, out of the blue, he asked me whether I knew Daughtie Lourens. I had never heard of her, she'd not been in the camp. That's when Jack showed me the picture. He said it had been taken earlier in the year, I think in January or February, it must have been at the time I was in the cave, when he was with a group of Khakis on commando somewhere in the southern Free State. One afternoon at sunset a captain and a few riders came back from patrol, and he walked out of his tent when he heard the horses' hooves. With them was a Cape cart and an emaciated mare and on the cart sat two ancient Boers and a young girl, probably around fifteen years old. That was the Daughtie he'd mentioned, the young girl. And she was there with the two old warriors with drooping shoulders who sat fidgeting on the cart.

That young girl, Jack then realised, was bent over because her hands were tied to the splashboard.

Then Jack showed me the photograph, he took it from a tin inside his camera bag. It's not a big photograph, but it's very sharply focused. She stands at the cart and her gaze is direct. She looks furious, but there is also something else. The captain has told her he'd take her to the camp at Springfontein, that's where the Khakis had just caught them, they were in their cart on the open veld with hardly any food and just the clothes on their backs. And then the captain said to the girl – she was fierce, said Jack Perry, like a small lynx – he said that he would take her back to the camp. She then said she refused, she wouldn't go, she'd just run away from that camp. She spoke to him exactly like that. It was then that the Khakis tied her hands to the splashboard.

That's the story that Jack told me. Jack had asked for her name and whether he could take a picture of her. That's the picture he showed me. I didn't look at it for very long, I didn't want to. Her hair hung wild and matted, and she seemed to be wearing just a petticoat. I don't know why I thought this, but it was good that they'd caught her, she deserved it, she was sinful and dirty. That's why I didn't want to look at the picture.

I didn't say anything, just looked away, and Jack put the photograph back in the tin. Then we didn't speak again for a long time. He just said that he'd had the picture developed at Caney's studio in Kimberley. That's all. I wanted to say to him that she deserved it, but I didn't.

I thought about all those soldiers at Matjiesfontein walking towards me, and I'd said nothing, just felt vaguely guilty. Yes, I felt guilty that Daughtie or whatever her name is, that she'd been caught and not I, because I know I'm just as guilty as she is.

Perhaps Jack Perry and I spoke too much. It was improper, shouldn't have happened. Who am I to be chitchatting with Jack Perry? Who am I?

"Come," Jack said, "let me show you where the lavatory is, then I'll go and fetch my luggage while you're busy."

There he goes and says that word! And here it is, written on the door: *Lavatory for Ladies*. I quickly look away.

"Wait for me here at the entrance," Jack says. "Please don't walk around; I'll never find you again."

Here I stand. It looks a lot like the one at Bloemfontein, except that there's a mirror here. The last time I saw myself was in the cave, in the mirror that Tiisetso gave me. Without the cap. My hair long and wild and loose, and when I brushed it to the side, the scar from the cut was there, there where my hairline starts and it ran deep across my scalp. Now the cap hides everything. She could at least have worn a bonnet, that Daughtie Lourens. At least my head was covered when that damned Khaki at Bloemfontein station leered at me like that.

Jack is already waiting outside. We push through the crowd. He struggles to carry all his belongings. Outside in the street, at first I am blinded by the bright light and there's a very strange smell. It stinks. Jack looks at me and says: "I've thought about it again and I now know where the best place is for you."

He starts walking again. "Come," he says, "it's not far. Just here, up this big road; there, you can already see the house."

It's not far, but with all the luggage you might easily land under some wheels or the feet of the many soldiers around. It's a nest of Tommies, this Cape Town. There's a wide step up to a front door with small shiny panes. Jack speaks to someone who opens the door and then it shuts again. The air is full of noisy white birds. "Gulls," Jack says. "The sea is just behind us, can you hear it?"

I try to listen, but the door opens and we enter a hallway with a high ceiling, where a woman is waiting for us. She's fairly old, but she's strong, she's very strong, and she's wearing elegant clothes, smooth black velvet with a delicate white collar at her chin, her hair combed from a middle parting and pulled into a bun at the back, and on top of her head sits a little flat hat. Mrs Koopmans, says Jack.

The old woman looks at me and then at Perry. "Goodness, Mr Perry," she says, "when was the last time I saw you?" She speaks very good English. "It must have been when you took that picture of Princess ..." She says a name I can't hear properly and then Jack laughs and blushes. Mrs Koop-mans says the princess is very angry about the photograph. I did not think that this country had princesses; we don't even have a king. Mrs Koopmans turns to me and says: "Princess Radziwill," and she must have seen how I frowned, because she repeats: "Rad – zee – wheel. Oh, don't worry, you'll be hearing a lot about her yet." She leans towards me, puts her hand on my shoulder and looks at me with concern.

"Is something the matter, dear?" she asks, and before I can answer she takes me by the shoulders and makes me sit down on a bench against the wall. "My child, my dear child," she says, "you are deathly pale."

"That is actually why we are here, madame," Jack says. "She's an Afrikaner. She comes from the north."

The woman looks from Jack to me. "Where do you come from, my child?" she asks.

"Winburg," I say.

"The camp?"

I nod. I don't look at her. Jack looks at me, his chin pulled in. Behind him is a room packed to the brim with containers. Merchandise, it seems to me. "I can take refuge at Mr Perry's," I say.

She looks at Jack again, and he gestures with his hand. "Come," she says to me, "start at the beginning and tell me what your name is."

I tell her my name. Susan, I say, and then softly – I don't think she's heard it – I say: Draper.

She looks at me a while and then speaks to Jack: "Mr Perry, I do hope you don't mind, but you know how I concern myself with the fate of my countrymen in the war. I therefore think it would be to everyone's benefit if Miss ..." and she turns to me again, "what is your name again, dear?"

"Susan," I say.

"And your surname?"

I look at Jack, and he nods. "Draper," I say. "My name is

212

Susan Draper." I don't know why, but now Jack's face looks worried.

"Well, then," says Mrs Koopmans, "I think Miss Draper should stay here with me. Don't you agree, Mr Perry?"

Jack sighs as if he is relieved, and he signals with his hand that I should decide. Before I can respond, the elegant woman says: "Call me Aunt Marie, dear. My name is Marie Koopmans-De Wet."

Chapter 31

She knows what she has to say to Hurst, and when he responds to her knock on the door she is ready. He is almost as transparent as she remembers from their first meeting, with the morning light falling between the open curtains behind him. She has a clear idea of how she must appear to him as she takes the four, five steps to the chair at his desk. How were they described, those Boer women who refused to bow to the might of the British war machine? Magnificent in their contemptuous fury. She sees him draw back, but without fear. Perhaps apprehensive, though not without a hint of amusement around his mouth.

"I want to, I think I must, explain," she says.

"You mean what happened to Hamilton-Peake?"

"Of course not. I mean to me."

"To you?" He watches her attentively, they hold each other's gaze before he says: "I hope you do not feel in any way responsible for his death."

"That is partly what I would like to explain, but I'm fairly certain that it is not what you suspect."

"What I suspect ... Good, let me be honest. I thought about it long and hard last night. I'll tell you what I suspect, it may make things easier for you."

"No, allow me …"

"It's the South African connection?"

"Please, allow me …" He knows! He has known since the beginning. Is that why he asked her? It's as if she is instantly drained, from her shoulders, through her arms and her fingertips.

"You knew him," he said.

And you knew that, she thinks. And you used it. She leans forward in her chair: "Major Hurst!" She is alarmed by her own voice – so is he – and she continues in a more muted tone: "Please allow me to explain. I have … Will you please try not to help me?"

"Of course. I apologise."

"You are right. It has to do with the war in South Africa. After all, you saw on his service record that he was there."

Now she feels certain: Hurst knew what had happened, and he used it. She had underestimated him. He wanted to do away with Hamilton-Peake and that's why he involved her. He knew! For a while she is too overcome to speak, yet eventually she manages: "You'd known it for a long time, hadn't you? You sent me to Hamilton-Peake knowing full well that I …" Then her thoughts become confused. It can't all be Hurst's doing. Hamilton-Peake is hers and hers alone. What happened happened between the two of them and no one else. Hurst must keep his hands off him.

It's as if Hurst's words are marching towards her through a sodden heath. "That, many years ago, you were on opposite sides in a war? No, I didn't know that when I asked you. And even if I'd known, why would I have wanted to use that fact? That you'd known each other … that I only deduced yesterday."

"Knew each other? What do you mean by that?"

"Perhaps you've already told me what you wanted to say, or what you needed to say."

She's regained some of her previous clarity. She'll have to play her cards right. "I should have expected an answer like that," she said. "You are, after all, a psychiatrist. That's also why I came to speak to you. I know enough about psychology to know that it's damaging to try to hide things."

She thinks she sees the beginnings of a smile on his mouth.

"I should have expected an answer like that from a Rivers disciple," he says. She is not going to outwit him very easily; she should have known that.

She begins hesitantly, feeling her way, her eyes appraising his throughout: "The facts are that I was in South Africa, during what your people call the Boer War – we prefer to make the actual aggressor part of the name …" Perhaps there was again a slight twist of the mouth, but again too slight to draw any inferences. "So, during the Anglo-Boer War I was in one of the concentration camps that your hero Kitchener built for women and children." She looks over his shoulder at the sunlight shimmering on the windowpane, vaguely aware that her words are lighter than she'd expected. "On the first of January 1902, when I was eighteen years old, the doctor in that camp signed my death certificate. Unofficially, I'd been murdered by two British officers and what we called a 'joiner', a Boer who fought on your side. But I wasn't yet dead, and I fell off the wagon that carted bodies to the morgue.

Some black people picked me up and saved my life."

That is all. Those are the facts. That is her story. Hers.

His lips hardly move when he speaks: "And Hamilton-Peake was one of those officers?"

"Yes."

"And did you kill him?"

Yes, she wants to say, I did; not you. But she knows it's not true. She too had spent the night wrestling with the events of the previous day, and what had led up to them, and when she'd knocked on his door a short while ago it was with the certainty that came from carefully retracing every stirring of her conscience. For a moment Hurst had put her off her stride, but now she has clarity again.

"No," she says.

"Would it have helped if you'd killed him?"

"I don't know. But that's not the question. The question is whether the fact that I'd seen him, whether that will help me."

"Now you no longer sound like a convinced Rivers disciple."

"And it sounds as though you don't pity me."

He looks at her impassively, does not say a word.

"I couldn't bear your sympathy," she then says.

"I know. I also know that he wanted to die, that's why he died. And that the question is rather whether you have enough sympathy for yourself."

Chapter 32

It was in Cape Town, where I got to know Aunt Marie, that my second life began. That's where I learnt to look at my life as if I were witnessing it from above, there in her house in Strand Street. Before that, I was wrapped up in my life like a baby in a blanket being carried on its mother's back. And it was at Aunt Marie's that I first got used to a city, however difficult it was and however strange it all seemed to me at first. Fortunately it wasn't necessary for me to go out, I could just stay inside Aunt Marie's house and sit in the sunroom, listening to her and her sister, Aunt Margaretha, talk to each other. When people came to visit – and there were constantly visitors – I usually went out to the back yard and chatted to the maids who hurried through the house all day in their white aprons, or I sat and stared up at the square patch of sky above me, high up, watching as the screeching gulls flew by.

At first I spent long periods just standing in the kitchen, breathing in all the smells and aromas, or sometimes lifting the lids off the pots and standing in a cloud of delicious steam, and then the head cook, Salomina, would show me what it was that smelt so good. She put this into my hand: a cinnamon stick, bay leaves, cumin seeds. And into my other hand she poured a spoon of turmeric or curry powder or masala. If there were not too many other people around, I went and sat with the sisters in the sitting room and feasted my eyes on the beauty, all the paintings, the glossy escritoire, the chairs and sofas with their shiny wood and velvet upholstery, the tall, delicately patterned porcelain, the soft carpet you could walk on noiselessly, and, by far the loveliest of all, the silver candelabra with its four arms holding slender white candles, and beside it a figurine, also silver, of a boy with a staff in one hand and his other hand raised as if to shield his eyes from the sun. Then I'd just sit there and listen to the two women talking – listening not so much to what they were actually saying, because I understood very little – and of the people they spoke about I only recognised a name here and there: Rhodes, Steyn, Kruger … It was especially the way they spoke, how their thoughts flowed into sentences that were strung together smoothly and rhythmically in a way that made me feel that everything one says should be done like that, no, everything should be done like that, and to speak like that, to listen and to show what you mean or how you feel with your body and your hands, that is something you should be able to do in order to live, to live well.

But the best, or perhaps it was just the first experience of my new life – or rather no, it was not – the ride in the softly swaying landau with its cushions that you could sink into, that was the first, with the silvery light and the wind against my cheek and the city's strange smells and sounds that echoed far more than in Bloemfontein and hung over you like a damp coat. But the very best thing about that first day

219

was when Aunt Marie took me to the bathroom in the late afternoon. It was the first time in my life that I'd seen a bathroom, the bath a big enamel tub filled with steaming water that was carried upstairs in buckets by the maids and there were curtains around the bath that you could draw closed.

Aunt Marie had a pile of folded clothing on her arm, which she began to hang from a rack in the corner. "Here are four dresses for you, dear," she said. "Choose the one you want to wear to dinner tonight. And I'll put some underwear on the chair for you, I think it should fit. Later, we can look at some shoes, hats and a jacket or two." She pointed to a towel, face-cloth and soap on a pure white marble top, then she smiled and pulled the door shut behind her.

And I was alone in that lovely, steaming bathroom with the smell of soap and flowers and the light linen curtains that you could pull closed and then sink down into the warm, warm water in a pool of white light. Every so often I try to reimagine how it felt that very first time, but it's as if it never really, really happened.

All too often when I try to recall lying in that bath, the first time or any time thereafter, I see myself lying in that cave again and looking up at the painting on the rock, and when I think of the voices I hear outside the bathroom door, the footsteps going up and down in the passage, I eventually only hear Mamello and Tiisetso's voices, then I remember Mamello soaping me down in the pool of rainwater and Tiisetso giving me the meerkat, and then I remember how in the camp we fetched water from the English at their water-cart, one bucket per tent per day, only one bucket.

In a bathroom full of steam like that you can cry without knowing whether it's steam or tears on your cheeks, and it doesn't really matter. I dried myself with a towel and chose a white dress with a ribbon that tied around the waist. It took a long time to dry my hair, but then I put on my shoes and went downstairs to where I heard the voices of Aunt Marie and Aunt Margaretha. That was the ninth of March 1902.

Chapter 33

She had to take the earliest train to Harwich to be in time for the mailboat back to the Netherlands. There was a seat at the window and now she sits staring at her reflection. There's a worried look on her face, almost anxious, as if her reflection is something she daren't look at, but also cannot tear herself away from. Oh, if only she could be more like Anne! Who would not have been in the least bit bothered by it all, whose mouth does not struggle so against its softness, who is less wide-eyed. If only she could look more like Anne.

It's dark outside. Sometimes a light flashes by, shadows that could be trees, the whiteness of a wall; she seldom recognises an actual shape, and it's not so much a result of the strange environment or the bad light, she soon realises, but because her thoughts are constantly unwinding, spooling back to her footsteps on another road, another railway track.

This morning Mrs Simms got up early to make her a last cup of tea. Jacobs was on time to take her to the station. Her time in England was over. Sooner than planned. But what was planned, and what had always been fated to happen in a preordained way? And if fate decreed that she should run into Hamilton-Peake in a hospital in Devon, then that has now been dealt with. But the journey, she knows, continues – the journey that started sixteen years ago in a dark coach on a pitch-black night, and a voice that came from the darkness, as if the night itself had spoken: "And so did you see what you wanted to see, Mr Perry?"

The other man did not answer immediately. "What I wanted to see, Doctor?" he said after a while, sighing audibly before answering: "It's hard to say. What did I want to see? I just do what my employer expects of me, and the commissioner in Cape Town wants photographs of British troops in action, and of a general state of siege. Useful photographs, if you know what I mean."

"Nevertheless, you were at the camp yesterday, not so?"

"Indeed."

"And?"

"I don't know, Dr Molesworth. It's very hard to say. You see something and set up your camera. By then you already have a picture in your head. Sometimes that picture is still there when you bend over to look through the lens. And sometimes not. Sometimes you have to ask people to stand up or lie down in a certain way. But most of the time you first have to look at the photo to know what it is you saw."

"But I mean now, Mr Perry. Your general impressions. All things considered."

The doctor's sentence was left hanging in the darkness. Perry did not answer. Molesworth remained silent. For a long while they just sat there jolting from side to side as the coach rattled on, the three of them, just vague outlines in the dark. Eventually the doctor spoke again.

"You know, Mr Perry, I probably didn't say this yesterday. Perhaps you know about it after all, news travels fast in a small place, and I'm now referring to the real reason I have to go to Bloemfontein." Perry still kept mum, and Molesworth continued. "Were you at the Show Grounds camp, Mr Perry? More than likely not. Alexander gave the guards instructions, I know. Here we call it the Show Grounds, the place for 'difficult cases', if you know what I mean, Mr Perry. My colleagues Dr Werdmüller and Dr Schnehage tell me that in other camps they speak of the ewe camp – Sister Bakkes will confirm this for you. A type of cage, you see. And it sounds terrible when you say it, but in Britain we also have this, the isolation and incarceration of those whose mental state makes them unfit for normal social interaction. We don't in fact have any other treatment for this, Mr Perry. But in a war, in another country, confronted by other cultures and other customs, you're forced to look at it differently. Alexander doesn't agree, but the fact is, he's the camp superintendent while I am the subordinate. Even as regards medical matters. That's why I'm going to Bloemfontein. I have to give an account of myself."

A man comes to sit across from her, glum under his dark hat, and she is back in the British train that is rattling through the inky darkness.

She becomes aware again of her reflection in the window, the weariness of her mouth. She looks away quickly. When she'd gone to say farewell to Hurst, he was standing at the window with his back to the door; turned around as she had entered. They both walked to the desk, each had stood behind a chair on either side of it, the desk like a battlefield between them.

"You did good work," he had said.

She'd examined his face, his eyes, for a clue as to what he meant. But his eyes were also searching, serious, troubled, as if wishing to assure himself that she had understood him. Was he referring to Hamilton-Peake? Dare she think that? And then she decided, there, in Hurst's sunlit office, and before he had a chance to pass judgement or to give his approval, right there, she took a grip on her life and said: "I killed him."

That is what she said: I killed him.

His expression did not alter. She saw his eyes searching, slowly swivelling two, three times, and then he softly spoke again: "I can attest to the fact that patients benefited on an ongoing basis from your understanding and empathy—"

She cut him short: "I killed him."

"... and your inspired application of psychological suggestibility," he said as if he had not heard her.

She did not repeat her statement. They stood silently watching each other. "Then the matter is closed," he eventually said, walked around to her and took her hand. "You have to believe that."

She looked down at their hands; his was paler than hers. Then she lifted her head, tried to smile, and let her hand slip from his.

She pulled Hurst's door shut behind her and remained standing there, her eyes closed in order to gather her thoughts. When she opened them again, her hand flew halfway to her mouth in fright, because a little farther down the corridor Anne was pulling a door shut behind her almost exactly as she'd done at their first meeting.

For a moment Susan considered pretending that she hadn't seen her. She would rather have seen Anne at the nurses' station or in one of the offices, alone, to take leave of her ... yes, if not privately, at least to make it more or less formal. But she was unable to free her gaze from the woman who, slowly and semi-preoccupied, pulled the door shut behind her and with that cool-headed expression started walking towards her.

"You're leaving," Anne said. Not asking, just stating a fact. She did not answer.

"Was it because of the patient in room 114?" Anne's eyes flicked towards Hurst's office, and as if provoked by her gesture, the door opened.

"Oh," Hurst said. "Here you are still." His eyes went from hers to Anne; she followed Hurst's gaze, and she saw how Anne looked at the doctor, knowingly, as if they were complicit, and then she knew what it was: Anne believed him and not her! She felt a fury rise up in her, like a wave against a harbour wall – her despairing wave against their wall – her despairing wave against their communal wall, their effort to take Hamilton-Peake away from her.

She swung around and walked away. Soon enough she turned a corner and was beyond the reach of their treacherous eyes, that devious conspiracy. Once in the courtyard she began to walk faster, the gravel crunching under her shoes. What on earth had made her think that Anne was on her side?

How could she have exposed herself like that? Here in the train, miles away already from that town, that hospital, she tries to understand what had happened there. Why had she reacted so strongly? But the farther the train rumbles away from that scene, the more unreal it becomes to her. She tries once more to retrace her steps. What precisely was it that infuriated her so about Hurst – and Anne, yes, especially Anne! How could she have suspected Anne? In a way, Anne had saved her life, and perhaps that's the reason: that she couldn't bear the fact that this woman who meant so much to her was suddenly in cahoots with Hurst. But what kind of nonsense is that? What sort of primitive jealousy?

She becomes aware again of her reflection in the window; the furrow between her eyes. I am alone now, she thinks, and that is how it should be. My life, the road I am on, is in my hands, and that is all that matters.

The thought brings a degree of comfort. The wild swirling in her mind subsides.

When she left the hospital, she still had to go and take leave of Mrs Simms. In the kitchen, she watched her landlady's face over a cup of tea. For some reason Mrs Simms still seemed pleased with herself, still wore that condescending smile. Perhaps the woman really does know something I don't know, she thought, and purposefully put her cup down and quickly got up.

"Probably for the best," Mrs Simms said, "that you'll be getting away from that …" She waved her hand above her head as if she were chasing away flies, and Susan barely managed a polite smile.

When, minutes later, Jacobs dropped her off at the station, Susan's thoughts were still occupied with Mrs Simms's all-knowing smile, and again, as they so often had in the short while she'd known her landlady, her thoughts focused on the impression she'd given of seeing someone standing behind her. It's more than just an impression, she thought, it's an unsettling feeling, a sudden idea, a hunch. As she greeted Jacobs with her hand held out to him and he giggled nervously, toothily, with a grating sound in his throat, it suddenly dawned on her. Right there. She stiffened, and it was as if she were looking through him and seeing something else – someone else, behind Jacobs. And Jacobs looked around, over his shoulder, and then again back at her. Confused.

"Will you give Dr Hurst a message?" she said.

His top lip pulled up over his front teeth. Like a ram, she thought again. By then she could think this, she saw everything clearly, in full control of her faculties.

"Tell him there was another one."

"Just that? Another one?" Jacobs lifted his shoulders and widened his eyes as if he were talking to a child or an idiot.

"Yes," she said and turned around. "There was another one." She took a few steps away from him, then turned again to face the young orderly who stood watching her with a sheepish grin. "Tell him there were two," she said, and walked towards the waiting train.

Here, in this rocking train, it is hard for her, almost impossible, to recall anything of that moment. Or why she had said that.

It was as if her thoughts were hurtling along with the train

228

towards another destination, towards the dawn of a new day, and away from the fathomless darkness she'd so long been journeying through.

Chapter 34

Aunt Marie is sitting at the head of the long yellowwood table in the dining room. She and Aunt Margaretha looked at me with a smile when I entered. A place was set for me on the left of Aunt Marie. They waited for me to sit down, and then they seemed to wait for something else, both kept looking at me. Aunt Marie leant forward and waved away a fly that was circling the table, then she sat down again and put her hand on my arm. "Susan, *my hartjie*," she said, "won't you please take off your tam-o'-shanter? Around here we don't wear hats at table. A bit of ribbon or a scarf would be fine ..."

What is she talking about? It feels as if my heart has just fallen with a plop from my chest. I look at Aunt Margaretha.

"Your hat," she says, and points at my forehead with a jab of her finger, "the cap you're wearing."

Something in my head begins to buzz. I look at the two women, but I can't see them clearly. My hat? I am wearing a hat, the one that Jack Perry gave me in Bloemfontein. Slowly the picture becomes clear to me. I've been wearing the hat ever since it was given to me. Only once, for a short while in the bath, have I taken it off. I didn't know it then, but I do know it now: There was only one way I could leave Tiisetso and Mamello's cave, and that was with a hat that covered my head.

"Aunt ..." I begin, but my throat is too dry to speak.

She squeezes my arm; her hand has been there all the while. She pushes her chair back and comes to stand behind me.

Before me is just the white of the plate, a blinding white. She slowly pulls the hat off my head and my whole body becomes as rigid as a rifle butt. Her fingers slide into my hair and comb it back. Her hand lightly brushes my forehead and slowly feels its way up again. I begin to cry, see my tears fall. I see Mamello looking up at me, her eyes as milky as the soapy water in the rock pool filled with rain. Aunt Marie's fingers are in my hair, her fingertips soft on my scalp. "My child, *my hartjie*," she says, "What did they do to you?" I hear Mamello say: *Ngwana wa ka*. And it feels as if they are here with me again, Tiisetso and Mamello together with Aunt Marie and Aunt Margaretha, and I am their child.

Aunt Marie's voice seems to come from far away, as if she is standing in the mouth of the cave and I am far back in its darkest corner. She says I must try to live without the hat, otherwise the scar will continue to be the most important thing in my life. "Do you have any family?" she asks. "Where are your mother and father?"

"Dead," I say. "My mother and brother both, in the camp. My father on commando."

"And the rest of your family?"

"We were bywoners," I say, "sharecroppers in Ermelo, where I grew up. My father worked with horses, he broke

231

them in. Then we got a place on a farm near Heilbron. That was before the war. Pa left with the Kroonstad commando from Uncle Thys's farm."

"And you were taken to the Winburg camp?"

I just sit there. Aunt Marie's hands rest lightly on my shoulders. Aunt Margaretha sits listening with her head down. She doesn't look at me, she just looks at the table.

I tell them about the Scouts who shot our dog when they came to fetch us. Me and Ma and Neels were standing by the covered cart that we'd loaded up with a few of our things. The dog was tied up and it kept barking and jumping up. Chicken and goose feathers were all over the yard. Ma's white curtain blew in and out, in and out at one of the windows. The one Scout – he was a Boer like Olof Bergh, but at that stage I didn't yet know him, it was the first time I'd seen him – he came walking out the door and emptied the last bit of paraffin left in his can onto the doorframe. There were no other sounds, nothing, nothing, nothing, just the barking of the dog.

I tell them about Alice who was so ill, so terribly ill. And the people who celebrated New Year, with the music and the singing that was so loud you could hear nothing else. I tell them how I walked between the tents to fetch her medicine and how someone had grabbed me. I tell Aunt Marie that something bad happened to me. I tell her it was a joiner who also came from Heilbron and two English officers. I knew them. And I knew their names. But I didn't have a name for what they did to me. That I still cannot say.

Then I keep quiet. I don't know how to tell the rest. I saw

232

all of it, like it came to me in the cave. At first it came blowing towards me like the smoke of a dung fire, in streaks, and then it was gone and I was so scared of it that I wanted to die. But I have never said it. I don't know what the words are. I will have to stay here with Aunt Marie to learn the words, and how they fit into sentences, so that those sentences can en-wrap what I see inside my head and feel inside myself, so that it becomes something that I can put down in front of other people and say, look, this is what it was. Look, here I have put it down between us, on the ground, don't get a fright, it won't cause any harm.

All that I'm able to do is tell Aunt Marie and her sister about the cave. About the coach. About the train. About Tii-setso and Mamello. About Jack Perry. That is all I'm able to do. And then I tell them that my name is Susan Nell, and that I have taken Alice's surname. That my real surname is Nell, but that it was easier to make my way with Alice's surname, because of the war. And because Alice was probably dead.

Aunt Marie's hands slide from my shoulders to my arms. "Take back your name," she said. "You are Susan Nell. That's the only way to start living again, by taking back your name. It's a start."

Chapter 35

It was raining when she arrived in Dordrecht. Soft, European rain that fell straight down from low clouds, pricking the smooth reflections of rooftops and gables. She'd walked some distance under an umbrella over a thin membrane of water, each footstep a jolt that dissolved this whole lovely lustrous scene into rippling rings. And it felt good.

When she rings the doorbell at the practice, it is Reymaker himself who opens the door. Strange. She gives a quick smile and turns her back on him to close the umbrella while also attempting to regain her composure.

"Straight from the trenches!" he greets her, steering her inside and guiding her to his office. The receptionist is ill and the assistant nurse, the one who has taken over from her, is in the clinic at the back.

He takes his place behind his desk, smiles broadly, his lips clamped together. He is happy to see her. "You're in one piece," he says, "that's the most important thing."

She sits down. "My room at least is still in one piece," she says rather pointlessly, but she needs a preamble, she needs to find her feet. "I quickly went to drop off my luggage."

He keeps watching her with that feline smile, slit-eyed and

attentively nodding. It's as if she's describing how she'd dragged a Bergonic chair, complete with distribution board, generator and the bird's nest of electrical cords up the stairs of her apartment. She'll have to tell all.

"I've been in the wars," she says.

"The war, yes," he says.

"But I ... I mean I was in one myself," she says.

"Yes, you," he says. "I think I know what you're saying. And you are in one piece?"

"Before I left, you said it was the war that attracted me. Do you remember that?"

"That is exactly what I said."

"Were you aware that my war was not yet over?"

He stands up, the smile gone, staring at something behind her.

She looks around; he walks past her and pulls a book from a bookcase that covers the entire wall behind her. He gives it to her.

"You'll have to learn German," he says and sits just behind his cat statuette. "Freud," he says. "The things you thought were in the past."

She reads the title: *Zur Psychopathologie des Alltagslebens.* She'll first have to learn German. She wipes a palm across the cover, and then the letters begin to swim before her eyes. She looks away quickly, to the side, so that he won't notice her distress. Now where does that come from? She wipes at her eyes with her sleeve.

"First you must get some rest," Reymaker says, getting up and walking over to her. "We'll talk again tomorrow. A good

235

night's rest makes an enormous difference, Freud will tell you that too." He gives a short, dry cough and accompanies her to the front door with the swaying gait of an old man, clearly chuckling to himself.

This time, as she's about to unlock the apartment door, something occurs to her. Jacques. She looks over her shoulder; his door is shut. Of course, what did she expect? Still, she walks to his door. Maybe there's something. A letter or a parcel. A notice. Some or other sign. But there's nothing. She sniffs at the door, only because she is standing so close to it. She shudders. Lowers her nose until her forehead rests against the wood.

Then she hears it, a sound from inside. It sounds like a broom against a skirting board. And again. She holds her breath. Something is being moved across the floor. Footsteps. There is definitely someone inside.

She knocks. Hesitantly. Too softly. She knocks again.

The door opens, and before her stands a woman who wipes her hands on her apron. Youngish. A strand of hair falling over the round face.

"Sorry, I'm looking for Jacques," Susan says. "Jacques la Mer."

The woman tucks the hair behind an ear. "The previous owner?"

Previous? Only a month ago he was still here. Or rather, the place still belonged to him.

"He's gone," the woman says. "We live here now." She looks over her shoulder as if she wants to call someone; turns around again, her face pulled back. "He died," she says. "In the war. That's what they told us."

236

It takes a second before Susan registers properly. He is dead. Yes, that is completely understandable. Dead. In fact, the logical consequence of it all. What else might she have expected? "I'm sorry to have bothered you," she says to the woman, and turns around.

She feels strangely light walking back, as if she wants to free herself from the earth. Light and cool and completely empty of thought.

She pushes the key into her lock, hears Jacques's door slam shut behind her, and turns the key. She tries to concentrate on every detail of what she is doing: the turning of the doorknob, the slight effort needed to push the door open, the dainty click of the latch behind her.

She sits down at the small table in her empty room. Waits. She waits for something to come to her. To remember something. To feel something. For a long time she sits like this in the slowly darkening room. Motionless she sits, until even her unease at her numbness dissipates and nothing is left but the silence.

Chapter 36

She catches a tram not too far from the front door of the house belonging to Mrs Koopmans-De Wet. She knows where to go and she knows how to get there. She bends down low in the car, peering through the window to see the flat top of the mountain with its ever-fraying skirt of clouds. As she bends, she can't help but notice too the tips of her new red-brown shoes below the hem of her dress. Her new shoes! She snorts with laughter, feels a delicious sense of anticipation as she hangs from the roof handle and surrenders to the rush and tumble, the crush of passengers, the scraping of women's hats, the strange mixture of smells – tobacco is the only one familiar to her. Occasionally the city wafts in – horse manure, smoke, innards, rotten fish, the sea … but she's grown accustomed to it, all part of the mystery of this city, this pile of concrete and metal that's torn between the gifts of the mountain and the sea.

At dawn she'd lain listening a while to the gulls, then to the first clatter of vehicles, and then to the street voices. The bay had been blown full of ships, their masts like thorn-tree branches stacked up to protect seedlings from chickens. She'd found the two sisters in the sitting room among crates and heaps of clothing and shoes, along with three other women unpacking and sorting into piles. Aunt Marie was sitting on a piano stool, pointing and giving instructions. "Come here, Susan," she said as soon as she saw her. "Good morning, did you sleep well? I want to introduce you to the women you'll be working with from next Monday." She'd hardly shaken hands with them when Aunt Margaretha directed her towards a row of shoes against the wall. "Choose what you need, Susan, then we'll take whatever is left over."

While she was standing there, deciding about some shoes, her dress and petticoat around her legs, her hair curling over her forehead, Aunt Marie's voice came from behind: "Susan, Margaretha tells me you're reading Vondel."

What does the old woman mean? She'd seen the book on the shelf; the one her father had given her was burned with the farmhouse. She knows parts of *Lucifer* off by heart: Is it fate that I will fall, robbed of honour and dignity, Then let me fall, if I were to fall, with this crown upon my head …

"That's what's given me this idea, and I've already spoken to Margaretha about it."

She hurries down Plein Street now, faster and faster, driven by excitement. She'd seen the signboard from the tram, and occasionally from the landau too: *Perry's Photographic Services*.

He is bending over a table at the back of the shop, and comes slowly upright; with him is a smartly dressed young man with an extravagant moustache and a silly strip of beard on his chin. Jack immediately stretches his arm out to her, welcoming, surprised; the other man looks down at her from a height. For some reason she looks down at her new shoes, and when she looks up again, both men are still standing there staring.

239

Then in a high-pitched voice the young man takes his leave of Jack and, without looking at her, walks out.

She and Jack greet each other, and Jack says something – something kind – about her appearance and the two of them go and sit in a corner of his shop, she babbles on excitedly, mainly to mask their mutual discomfort, the discomfort about what had happened, the history, her story. Almost in astonishment, he sits listening to her, occasionally somebody comes in, looks at the furniture or photographs on display, though it's unnecessary for him to get up. And then she grows quiet, as if the spring inside her has uncoiled, he does not say anything, and she says in a hushed voice: "There's an opportunity for me to go to the Netherlands."

He tilts his head as if he has not heard properly, but then his eyes crinkle in amusement, and she tells him about Mrs Koopman's efforts to arrange a bursary for her to study overseas.

"Overseas? Why not here? There are opportunities here too, you know."

She does not know. It never occurred to her to question Mrs Koopmans's proposal. She was perfectly happy to continue doing what she was doing now indefinitely, namely helping to send clothes and food to the concentration camps, but when the good woman spoke about the possibilities, about her Dutch family who could initially provide lodgings, the thought germinated and irrepressibly grew in her.

"I don't know," she says, slightly taken aback, looking down at her hands, waiting, and then she quickly looks up at him again. "Maybe she thinks it's a good idea for me to go away."

"Do you know yet what kind of training you'll receive?"

She does not know. Aunt Marie said she could decide for herself what she wanted to study. She didn't have enough schooling to attend a university, the war had seen to that. Is that what Jack thinks, that she is too uneducated? That she's a bywoner's child, a war orphan. She tries to read his eyes, and he looks down at something he's been holding in his hands all this time.

"What's that?" she asks.

"At least you have enough self-confidence now," he says.

"That thing in your hand," she continues, "what is it?"

"A photo," he says, "of the man who was here when you came in."

He holds the picture out, and she casually looks it. He's actually still a youngster, she again realises, as he lounges in a chair, his left elbow on the backrest. He looks past the camera with that idle, haughty air of his.

"He doesn't like the picture," says Jack.

"Why didn't you help him fold his handkerchief properly?"

"The last time I showed you a photo you didn't like it either," he says.

She looks at him sharply. He gazes at her calmly, unwavering. "What does a person see in a photo?" he then says. "What is it that attracts or repulses one?"

She remembers the bleak landscape through a train window, the girl at the Cape cart, that direct, challenging, fearless look. "It wasn't a photograph of myself that you showed me," she says.

"I know," he says.

241

There is something else in that photo, the one of – what was her name again? – Daughtie, yes, now she remembers the name, but that impression, she knows, lies shallow in her memory, just below the soil, ready to be snatched up, like assegais planted there with a purpose. It's the whoreishness of the girl. That's what it is. Perry knows it too, she's certain of that. He knows. She turns her eyes to him carefully, warily, but he is looking at the picture in his hands and not at her. "Why did this man not like his photo?" she asks.

"Perhaps he saw what you saw now."

"Is it then something that he didn't know, about himself?"

"Photos – good photos – are about more than what you see on the surface."

"You purposely left his handkerchief bunched up in his jacket pocket and his tie awkwardly tied and made sure everyone could see his big Boer hands."

"You suddenly know a lot about photography," he says, and then with a wry laugh: "And about psychology."

"Psychology?"

He nods.

"What is it, psychology?"

He looks at her from under knitted eyebrows, his elbows resting on his knees. "It's the art, no, the science, of discovering what goes on inside people. In your heart, your head. Your soul, one might say. What's wrong there, and how to fix it. It's something you could study towards. You'd become a kind of doctor." Behind him, the late afternoon sun slants into the shop window, and everything outside – the pedestrians, bicycles and coaches – are momentarily suspended in the glow, as in a photograph. For a while she sits stupefied. "Thank you," she then says, past Jack's head and into the light. "Thank you very much, Jack," she says.

Less than a month later she was on the foredeck of the *Glenart Castle* en route to the Netherlands. She would study psychology. There would be opportunities. A new life. Behind her, like far-off cannons firing, the waves thundered against the rocks of a godforsaken continent.

Chapter 37

She went back to South Africa only once. She'd just turned seventy, and finally called it a day at Reymaker Psychiatrie. After the massive upheaval of the Second World War, life in the Netherlands carried on as normal, quiet and calm, like the Oude Maas flowing past her rooms. She returned the same way she'd arrived fifty-two years previously, taking a passenger ship to Cape Town and then a train to Bloemfontein. The only difference was that they travelled to Winburg by car.

Only once, while aboard the ship, did she think: I am going home. I'm going home at last. Just that – just the thought. No accompanying stir of the emotions, none at all. She had stood waiting with the wind in her face; waiting for the thought to crystallise into a definite meaning, but it seemed destined to remain insubstantial, a wisp of smoke blown away by the wind. There were tears in her eyes, but it was the wind, nothing more.

Was it because the thought had been so unexpected? She had indeed seldom thought about it like that. She cannot remember that she'd ever, during all her years in Europe, longed for home. In any case, what would "home" have meant for her? Perhaps a cave somewhere in the Free State. Yes, exactly: something as small and claustrophobic as a cave. That was, after all, where this life of hers had begun. And to return is to go back from whence she came, back to the womb. Anyone who knows anything about psychology would know what that means. But in her case it was a bit more complex. If you hanker for the beginning, it is a veiled death wish, they say, but were her end and beginning not switched from the outset? What should have been her grave was her birthplace.

She turned her back to the wind and folded her arms in front of her, lowering her chin to her chest. Three wars later, and here I am, she thought. I am going home, the wars are over. That is perhaps all that going home means, that the war is over. My father was one of the first to fall in the wars fought by the Boer Republics against England. And I went to the Netherlands. But then a pimply Serbian teenager stuck a gun into the neck of a moustached Austrian nobleman and pulled the trigger. The start of the Great War. Not twenty years later, and this time not a pimpled face, but Hitler. And the strangest thing of all is that it seemed so natural to her, all that terrible suffering, that insanity.

Ever since that moment that she'd stood – she was actually just a child still – on that stinking Cape wharf among the screeching gulls, shouting porters, seamen and soldiers, and the moaning of ship horns, feeling confident and excited, she had left herself and everything familiar behind. Almost three weeks later the ship sailed into the solemn silence of Amsterdam's harbour, and she herself walked into a world that she could scarcely have imagined: the moist air, the sharply pitched roofs, the shadows falling across tranquil waters, and people calmly making their way through that world, completely aloof, as if behind glass. And she thought: That is how it should be. One can live like this, in this absolute foreignness, with complete detachment.

Until the Great War broke out and something cracked inside her like ice. She went to Devon, to that shellshock hospital. There was the episode with Hamilton-Peake, as if fate had decreed it. And that crack deep inside her was forced open to let the light in. She had recovered, and she ensured that the light also brightened the lives of others. That is what her career as psychotherapist enabled her to do, and during the Second World War ... and yet, and yet ... yes, there was something.

It is actually part of one long story, she has known that for a long time. It can't be divided up into three wars, because it is her story: It is my story. I am at home in it. That's what caused all the fuss with Hurst back then. How long did it take her to figure it out? A year? More? The fact is, she felt that Hurst wanted to rob her of the opportunity to claim back her story. She and no one else would be its author, especially not a man. And in her story Hamilton-Peake belonged to her, *she* would decide what happened to him.

That's all she was granted, a story. That's also what she had told Lucille, the Javanese war orphan, when she'd found her, completely crushed, at the Kwai River Tribunal. And afterwards, that's what she kept repeating to her: see to it that you are the creator of your own story. And she, Susan, made damn sure that Lucille knew *her* story, the story of how she was picked up from the bare veld next to the concentration camp … So that she might know, and take comfort. So that both of them might live.

Perhaps your home, the place you call "home", is just a story. Or at least, then, it is the place where your story unfolds. And there are some stories that can only unfold in one place and nowhere else. That place is that story's home. And if that story is yours, then that place is also your home.

In fact, her story has been told. Only the end is missing. But she does not want to think about that now, that is not how she lived her life, with death in mind. No, on the contrary. And why should she spin herself into a cocoon of dark thoughts?

She rose to her feet and sought comfort in one of the ship's brightly lit halls, among passengers who always looked as if they'd just been summoned to the captain's quarters. But before she was swept up in the colourful commotion, the clatter of footsteps and the thrum of voices, there was still one last thought: If I am now searching for the appropriate setting to end my story, is it not the case that my ends and beginnings have always been switched around?

Jack Perry at least was still at the Cape. He is in his early eighties, his wife died almost a decade ago, and their only son manages the Bloemfontein branch of Perry's Photographic Services. Through sporadic postcards, with now and then a letter, she's kept up to date with the superficial details of his life. Sometimes he'd sent photographs, and so the physical evidence of the passing of time was not a great shock to her. He is old.

The country – the Cape – was, however, utterly alien. All

she recognised was the sea, the waves, the mountain. She remembered some of the street names. She was on the point of asking the taxi driver to take her along Strand Street, but for a while she was completely disorientated, and by the time she recovered they were already well on their way to Jack's house in Rondebosch.

Now they are sitting across from each other in the dining car of the train en route to Bloemfontein. She doesn't really know why he insisted on accompanying her. Perhaps because he was the only one who was present when it all began. Or where it ended, she thought wryly. Perhaps he felt responsible, in a paternal way. The age gap between them has grown, and like a grey-haired father, he sits opposite her, drumming stubby fingers on the white tablecloth, making noises in his throat, and seemingly lost in thought. Outside lies the open veld; next to the tracks, occasional silver-white plumes of grass, black rock strewn on bleached red soil that has washed away here and there to reveal grey-green and rust-brown layers of gravel. Eventually she manages to turn away from the empty landscape, though still aware that it is *there*, the terrifying expanse. Her eyes on the upholstery, she wonders, is that how I experienced it when I travelled down this track all those years ago? Was it so frightening to me then, this emptiness, that time I was in the grip of death? Or has it lain in my subconscious all these years, the knowledge that *this* was what awaited me here?

That is perhaps what prevented me from returning, or even longing for home. Precisely because I grabbed hold of life so desperately. I could not on pain of death afford to long for home. Only in the Netherlands, in an alien place, could I create a story in which I felt at home. My story. But now, intensely aware of the never-ending, shimmering emptiness around her, she also knows that to live in a foreign country is to inhabit a narrative, to live in an illusion, a manufactured reality. Even though it was her only way of surviving.

She questions him as closely as she can. Perry does not talk about his life easily, she's already realised that. The question about the loss of his wife he answered with a mere shrug and a pained laugh. But when he speaks about the country and the changes it has undergone, life under a new government – "your people" – then he speaks enthusiastically, sometimes even angrily.

What was there to say about her life? It had mainly been work. She limited the narrative to her last big project, when she was called as an expert witness at military tribunals for atrocities committed by Japan in the Second World War. She spoke about Lucille. How she'd taken her under her wing and how they'd remained friends and were in regular contact.

He listens intently, with one hand resting on the table top. "And you became a psychiatrist," he said. "Remarkable, absolutely remarkable."

"Psychotherapist," she says. "And it was you who put me up to it."

"Me? Come now, that can't be the case. It was Koopmans-De Wet, if I remember correctly. Yes, it was she."

"Yes. Without her it couldn't have happened. But what I'm referring to is the idea of being trained in the field of psychology."

"Oh, yes," he said, "psychology. But psychiatry; that's a completely different matter, not so?"

"Yes, and it happened because I had to learn German in order to read Freud. And having learnt German, and a little bit about Freud, I went to Germany to study psychotherapy."

"Remarkable, absolutely remarkable." He looks past her, up in the air, pensive. "But you never married," he said. "You never said anything about that."

She does not answer immediately; gazes into his virtually immobile eyes, slightly droopy like those of a beloved old dog. Harmless, she thinks, don't upset yourself, but she remains apprehensive, and decides to ignore the comment. "It all began in fact in that cave near Winburg," she says. "Do you remember me telling you about it?"

"I can imagine something like that putting one off the mere thought … Yes, the mere thought."

It takes a while for her to tease this out, as if her subconscious is actively resisting it. Then it dawns on her: those gentle dog-like eyes are entirely deceptive. She draws her nails over the cotton tablecloth and resolutely continues her narrative. All that matters is where it all began, and what, at the time, determined the direction it took. That, after all, is the only story you can tell in this country, the story of the beginning.

"And then you came," she says coolly, her eyes on her fist on the table top. She tries hard, but she cannot control this wave of resentment that suddenly overtakes her. "And I don't know what it was, but now I find the very idea repugnant, this effort to look into other people's souls." She is aware of having taken his words and sending them in a different direction, that she is turning his own words against him, but she simply doesn't have the energy to talk about her love life or the lack thereof. "Oh, those were probably just the things of a child. Childish fixations." Her voice is controlled again. "But it's those things that remain with you your whole life. They determine your life, in ways that you could never have foreseen."

He gazes at her, quietly and thoughtfully, as if he understands everything and also nothing. But then it strikes her that she herself is unsure of which fixations she's talking about: the way she grabbed hold of life when it was offered to her, or the way she could never rid herself of the seed of death in her heart.

When he begins to speak, he looks out of the window, and as his sentence unfolds he slowly turns his face towards her. "You wrote to me then …" Slowly, he nods his head, as if to urge on his own words. "That you …" he coughs, his fist at his mouth, then he pulls his eyes away and back again, "the rapist, you know … I mean the other one, the second one, that you also came across him?"

She realises now that his nodding is an attempt to soften his words, a gesture to temper the candour of the question, to rein it in, to relativise it.

She looks him in the eye; he looks away. Should she tell him? It's easy, she knows the words. She had told Lucille. Ensuring that she understood every last detail, to see clearly. But why would she tell him? He doesn't need it. Lucille, yes, she needed the story. More even than she herself needed it. Perry?

What good would it do him? It is the story of the end of a man's life. Ha. Nothing at all. He is in that phase of his life where he'll start dreaming about the very beginning, when he could still look the world directly in the eye and be absolutely certain of what he was seeing.

"Did I?" she said eventually. Only that.

He turns his face away from her towards the gently rolling landscape they're passing through, towards shades of green and khaki, cloud shadows on the grass, black children waving, a bundle of wood on a woman's head slowly turning as she stares at the train.

And suddenly, as if she were unaware of approaching Bloemfontein, the houses, hedges and garden gates, the sparse trees of the suburbs, flash past the window, like garbage spread along the tracks: brittle, colourful and completely heedless. As the train gives a final convulsive shudder between the platforms, she and Jack remained seated a while, half-dazed; she herself even a bit anxious. Jack grabs the window frame, pulls himself towards it as he looks out for his son who is coming to fetch them.

She walks ahead down the corridor, steps uncertainly onto the platform, grabbing at a handrail, for a moment blinded by the bright light.

Could this be the same place? She freezes, tries to orient herself, but nothing looks familiar. This country has also become an illusion, she thinks. The only reality has always been the one inside me.

In the back of Jack Perry Jr's car she turns to look at the station again. She remembers a Victorian veranda, but now there is a neo-classical façade with … She snorts, and from the corner of her eye sees Jack turn too.

That ridiculous little bell tower, like a miniature penis! She sits up, smoothing her dress over her legs. Oh, the place is innocuous, and so small … Perhaps she is too used to European cities, and the city – the town! – that she has returned to is one that exists only in her memories, one she experienced as a young woman.

"What is it, Susan?" Jack asks with a sympathetic chuckle. "What did you see that was so funny?"

She doesn't really know what to say. "Oh Jack," she says with a sigh, and she hears a warm mellowness in her voice, and is somewhat amused by it. It's the first time since I arrived at the Cape that I've sounded like this, she thinks, so … so well-disposed? She looks at Jack and sees him watching her, equally amused. "I don't really know why I laughed," she then says, self-consciously rubbing her finger on the seat. "You know how things seem so huge and overwhelming as a child … yes, and when you see them again, years later, you can hardly believe you're looking at the same thing."

"Yes, yes, I know, I know," Jack says. "If I showed you pictures I took at the time in Bloemfontein … do you remember the wagons, the horses? Here," he gestures at the scene outside the window, "the horse manure lay this deep."

"Do you want to drive through the city?" young Perry asks, glancing over his shoulder.

"No," she says impulsively, and after a moment's reconsideration, she has made up her mind: "No, thank you. I think your father is exhausted, and I …" No, she does not say it, she does not say that she feels no need for it. All she says is that she'd rather settle in first.

It's not a long drive to Perry's house. It's a squat pale blue building with a veranda emerging from the red soil of a large open yard. Susan cannot imagine that you'd have houses like that in a European city. She also realises that young Perry is not so young after all. Unlike his wife, who is waiting on the veranda and steps down smartly on high heels to come and meet them.

Dinner is served early. The two toddlers who'd been summoned at the start of the meal to greet them politely are now sent off to bed, and shortly thereafter – they're still enjoying dessert – young Perry takes his father off to his bedroom. Susan is left alone with the woman, and after a while, when the only sound is the clinking of spoons against porcelain, Susan is the first to speak. And purely for the sake of conversation, she asks after the only Bloemfontein building she remembers from fifty years ago: an imposing sandstone edifice with turrets along the façade.

"Oh, that's the Old Presidency," the woman says. "But for the past few years it's been used as office space."

Not a particularly friendly woman, Susan thinks. Her voice is monotonous, her face unanimated. She blinks her blue eyes slowly behind wide lenses. Yet the face looks familiar to Susan. The woman, named Helen, looks down at her plate, flicks her limp hair over her shoulder, and in a studied manner brings a piece of yellow peach with custard to her mouth. After swallowing, she asks, "Have you been in Bloemfontein before? I understand you came from Holland?"

254

"I was in Bloemfontein once. A lifetime ago. Very briefly, with your father-in-law." She realises that this announcement, her wording, could give rise to all sorts of speculation regarding the relationship between her and Jack. She wants to say something by way of explanation, but thinks better of it. Why should she be concerned about this? It's completely ridiculous. "It's the reason we came," she says in a measured tone. "I wanted to see the places I knew as a child. Tomorrow we're going to Winburg."

"Were you in the concentration camp there?"

So, she knows, and has only pretended not to know. Susan looks at the woman sharply. "Yes," she says. "One of the lucky ones who survived it."

"And you don't hold it against us?"

"Who is the 'us' you're referring to?" She doesn't say it aggressively, but is nevertheless annoyed by the underlying assumption.

"I mean us English."

"But you are surely not British? You are South Africans. Free-Staters."

"Yes, of course. It's just that the city has changed so much in the last while."

"You mean …?"

"Ten years ago it was still an English city," Helen says, her rising intonation making this sound like a question; a clear indication that Susan should draw her own conclusions.

Susan pushes her plate away. Where does she know this woman from? She decides not to say anything further, either about the simple dessert or about Helen's remarks. The

conversation has taken a turn for which she has not the faintest appetite. This is not what she actually wants to say, it's
the last thing she has on her mind. She doesn't want to get
involved in the Boer-Brit thing in any way whatsoever.

"I had a friend in that camp," Susan says softly. She doesn't
know why she's just said that. As if she has a need to share the
intimate details of her life with this strange, sullen woman.
But now she must press on; she leans back against the chair
and looks upward as she speaks. "Alice Draper. Wholly
English. But she was in that camp because her family considered themselves to be Free-Staters."

Susan hesitates, she has realised that she had been on
the warpath again – completely contrary to her intentions.
"Free-Staters, not British," she adds listlessly.

Helen does not react, though. She simply says: "What happened to her?" Her voice still flat and disinterested.

Susan is relieved that Helen has not taken the bait, but
then she feels irritated once more by the woman's lack of
sympathy.

Alice. For a while I was Alice, she thinks. For a while I had
the name of a dead girl. "I'm not sure what happened to her,"
she says. "I never heard from her again."

Helen gets up and starts taking the plates away.

"She's probably dead," Susan says, but Helen seems not to
hear her; she continues clearing the table and carries the dishes
to the kitchen.

Susan remains at the table with a few unused pieces of
cutlery lying on the white linen tablecloth. She hears sounds
in the kitchen; somewhere in the unfamiliar house a door

closes. She thinks: all the implications and suggestions, all the underlying meanings and tension in my conversation with this young woman, it's probably something only I am experiencing; it is mine and no one else's.

It is all part of a story that only I understand, and one for which even this country and its people can no longer offer a context.

Jack drops them off in the early morning at the home of a certain Mr Marais. He apparently owns a reliable car and has offered to take them to Winburg. He was himself a child during the war, young Jack explains along the way. Too young to fight, but he still remembers a lot, and is eager to talk about it.

They stop in front of a gate with a wire fence. The house is set back in a yard full of fruit trees, vegetable patches and chickens. Two paved tracks lead from the gate to a lean-to on thin metal stilts. That's where the car is waiting, its fins gleaming in the morning sun.

Mr Marais comes walking towards them with bowed legs, and wearing a khaki shirt and trousers. He raises his dark green felt hat in greeting. "Pleased to meet you," he says to her, and then he greets Jack Snr and says in Afrikaans: "Oh, well, I'll just speak Afrikaans, then. Sit in front with me, then the lady can sit behind us."

"No, no," Jack protests, "I want Susan to sit in front. This is her trip, and I want her to be able to see everything clearly."

"Oh, all right then, all right," Marais says, holding the door open for her and then shutting it with a click.

She hears the tyres crunch over the gravel, feels the shadows of the cypresses and kareebome sweep over them.

"I understand the young lady was in the camp," Marais says to her.

She stiffens: This is the first time since her arrival that she's had to speak Afrikaans. When last did that happen? A full sentence, and not just single words or phrases. Behind her, Jack doesn't make a sound. "You can …" she begins, but then Marais interrupts her.

"Winburg, hey?" he says. "Then we'll have to go there." A finger resting on the top of the steering wheel shoots to the left, apparently in the direction of a street they should turn into.

"My name is Susan," she says. Stiffly, though not bothered by the severity of her tone.

"Susan," she hears him say; but she does not look at him. "Call me Piet," he then says.

"Piet," she says. The name explodes over her lips. Delicious. The word lies comfortably on the tongue. A word is like a spark shooting from a fire. She turns to Jack and deliberately speaks to him in Afrikaans, remarking what a nice car this is.

"Dis 'n lekker kar dié van Piet, nie waar nie, Jack?"

"Dis 'n lekker kar, Susan," Jack replies. *"Dis 'n baie lekker kar."*

Has she imagined it, or did Jack intentionally smear some English butter over the r's? On the train she heard him speak much better Afrikaans with the waiters. But she smiles, pleased with herself, with what she considers an authentic Afrikaans image: English butter.

The city lies behind them now; before them is the narrow

blue strip that is the great road to the north. This can surely not be the same country? she thinks. On either side, the land-scape unfolds, green hip-high grass waving in the wind – as if touched by an invisible hand. Marais' fingers keep shooting up from the steering wheel, either in emphasis or to point things out: landmarks, farms and farm roads. Every now and again she registers something, but mostly she just sits back in bewilderment. Could this possibly be the same country? Where does all this rippling grass come from? Where is the dust? The smoke? She sees mottled cattle grazing, egrets lazily taking flight. Here and there, black people standing next to the side of the road. She wonders what they're wait-ing for, but Marais doesn't even seem to notice them. She watches him, his eyes slits, lips drawn back as if in pain. She sees the blood-red feather in his hatband. She looks away, to the layered clouds on the horizon. *That* she remembers. Oh, dear God, the clouds – *that* she remembers!

"Man," Marais says, "and they run with their tails like this, like this, this, this ..." He demonstrates with a swivel-ling forefinger. Susan has no idea what he's talking about; baffled, she looks around to see if she can see anything tail-like, but nothing catches her attention. "Where?" She asks. "Where do you see this?"

"Winburg," he says, "back then." He doesn't look at her, doesn't see her confusion. "Winburg had a race track. There were the showgrounds, and then the race track."

She doesn't remember this. "Where were you then?" she asks. "Were you in the camp?"

"No, not in the camp, no," he says, "but I know. Because

that's where me and my little friend, Paultjie, we were still young, very young. And then when we wanted to go and watch the races ..." He interrupts himself, leans over sharply towards her, his finger pointing past her eyes. "Look, look, look," he says.

She sees it: a long-tailed widow bird flying low over the veld, snatched by the wind and being dragged along with it. The bird is blown down the vlei, like a black armband tumbling over the bewildered grass. She watches until she can no longer see the bird. To think that this was something special for this miserable Marais. She looks at him again. He's wearing his usual Boer grimace, the face that the men of this country present to the world. If it weren't for that pretty flame-red feather, she couldn't bear to look at him.

Close by the black bird she saw a handful of little stipples. The females, she knows. And suddenly it occurs to her: Anne Maxwell – that's who the Perry woman looks like! That's who that sullen young woman reminded her of. In all these years she'd never thought of Anne, and now, here in South Africa, here, where she is en route to a concentration camp graveyard, the memory of that capricious British woman suddenly surfaces. How attracted she had been to her – or rather, how dependent on the woman's utter composure.

Is that how my subconscious is warning me of what is to come? she thinks. And what is it that's anticipated? She tries to disentangle it: I am driving with two men to the place where my mother and baby brother lie buried. No, she must not try to fool herself: She is now driving towards her own grave that lies somewhere in this Free State veld, and she has no defences against it, none at all. Not hate, not love, nothing.

A road sign warns: Winburg. She grabs the handhold above her head. Turns around to the silent Jack Perry. He gives a weak laugh, leans forward and squeezes her shoulder. The landscape looks familiar to her, but the roads, the new tar road and a few wide gravel turn-offs confuse her completely. Marais turns down one of the roads. "Do you know how to get to the graveyard?" she asks.

"No, you know, with all these new roads ... I'll have to ask."

Marais pulls up to a black man standing at the side of the road and winds down his window. The man approaches respectfully, bends down and looks inside, frowning, his eyes jumping nervously from the driver to the passengers and back again. She immediately recognises the Sotho sounds; she almost leaps up when she recognises the words, the greeting ritual she still remembers so well. She looks at the man attentively, sees his earnestness, the bent finger before his mouth, the way he looks around in response to Marais' question, as if he were searching for something among the bushes along the road, then looking down, shaking his head and saying that he does not know.

It is all social convention, she knows, each gesture is an ancient one, but also not – the uncertainty, the subservience is unfamiliar to her. Is that what this white man demands of this Sotho person? Marais spoke to him without an iota of respect, as if to a child. The Boer closes the window, and the car lurches forward. She turns and sees the man walking through the cloud of dust, back to the roadside. She looks at Jack, but his eyes reveal nothing. The eyes of an old man, she thinks. Eyes that no longer do what the heart demands.

"There was also a camp for black people," she says. She is speaking with her face turned to the window, her mouth almost touching the glass. "Right next to ours."

"You'd always find them huddled together at the race track," Marais says.

"What are you talking about, Susan?" Jack asks.

"About Tiisetso and Mamello," she says.

"Who?" Jack asks.

"Kaffirs," says Marais.

"The people I told you about, Jack," she says. "The people who healed me all those years ago. Do you remember?"

She feels Marais' gaze on her. Then Jack's voice comes from behind: "It's so long ago that you told me … No, Susan, sorry, my memory is no longer what it used to be."

She wants to swing around to Jack, but Marais makes a clicking sound, and from the corner of her eye she sees one of his fingers shoot up.

She can see the town now, the church bell, the roofs of the houses. Where would the cave be? she wonders. She hasn't the faintest idea. Even the church looks strange to her. She closes her eyes, aware of her breathing, in and then out again.

Marais is talking, here, next to her. "That boy said he thinks it's here, next to the town's rubbish dump." He stops, gets out, and opens a gate.

They are no longer in the town. He gets back in and drives carefully along a two-track path amid some long grass and the occasional bush. Then he comes to a halt. They sit a while in silence.

"I can't believe it," Marais says, and opens his door. He walks around and helps her and Perry out of the car. "Can't someone just ..." Marais doesn't finish his sentence. He walks among the overgrown graves, turns around to Susan and Perry who, somewhat helplessly, have both remained standing. "Do you know what you're looking for?" Marais calls to her.

Does she know what she is looking for? She turns to Jack who looks ahead with a frown. She follows his gaze, but does not notice anything in particular. She starts to follow Marais. Stumbling on shoes that are inappropriate for the veld.

"At least there's still one gravestone standing," Marais shouts.

She walks up to him, and reads the inscription on the pointed stone with its well-preserved engraving of a lily motif: *In loving memory of our sister Alice Alvina Rosie Draper. Died 6th Jan 1902*. She reads it over and over, as if her mind is unwilling to take in the words. Alice. It is Alice's stone.

She turns her back on Marais and on Alice's grave. Jack comes shuffling towards them. She walks past him blindly, vaguely aware of him putting out his hand to her, but she just keeps walking, her eyes on the horizon. The cave must be somewhere behind those ridges. She walks up and down through rough overgrown rows of neglected graves. In places some of the old numbers can still be seen, with here and there a legible gravestone. She walks farther and farther away from Alice's grave, shrubs grabbing at her shoes, grass whipping her shins, a blinding light in her eyes. My grave is also supposed to be here somewhere, she thinks, but where? My

God, my God … I died here, next to this rubbish dump, among this steekgras and those tiny scurrying ants, so small that you hardly notice them, so very small. And somewhere behind there, dear God, where? Behind there, up there in the ridges, there's a cave in the ridges, where I was born. My beginning and my end. Is that all? Is that all?

The return journey is mostly silent. After they left, Marais had remarked: "I hope you found what you came for," but she hadn't answered him. She couldn't. Total composure is always an illusion. An authentic end is always a complete surprise. A shock. Right to the marrow. Only later did she regain her composure.

At one stage Marais brakes suddenly and swings wildly to avoid a sheep crossing the road. The car leaves the tar, gravel scatters, the vehicle slides and tilts and Susan's head hits the window with a dull thud. Then the front wheels are on the tar again and the tail rights itself. Susan thrusts her hands against the dashboard; she thinks she may have screamed.

She feels her fingertips prickle and her left eye is watering.

Marais slows down and then pulls the car off the road. His lips are drawn back from his teeth and there is sweat on his nose and top lip. "Mastag-mastag-mastag," he mutters from below his hat with its bloodspot of a feather. She feels Jack's hand on her shoulder, warm against her neck. Then Marais reaches for her hand that had grabbed at her dress and scrunched it up. Two men reaching out for her and touching her gently, their hands resting on her warmly, comfortingly and protectively. For a while they just sit like that, the car making occasional clicking sounds and the clouds piling up in the darkening sky. "Just drive," she then says, and pushes their hands away, her eyes fixed on a distant point where the road tapers into the void. "Please, in heaven's name, just drive."

The Camp Whore is loosely based on the remarkable life of Susan Nell, as portrayed by Nico Moolman in his novel *The Boer Whore*. The manner in which Moolman came to hear about Susan Nell is in itself an extraordinary story.

On the evening of 7 August 2009, a Friday, Moolman was sitting in front of a computer in the Manohra Hotel in Bangkok. He was on a working trip – his import-export business necessitates frequent travel to the Far East – and he was typing a quick email to his daughter. Next to him sat his friend and business partner.

The doors of the nearby lift opened and an elderly Asian woman in Bermuda shorts stepped out. As Moolman passed an uncomplimentary comment on the woman's legs to his friend, she stopped, turned around slowly and walked up to him. "You are an Afrikaner?" she said.

Moolman was mortified, but the woman put him at ease and struck up a conversation. She said her name was Lucille, and that she came from the Thai city of Ubon. She had grown up in Java, hence her knowledge of Dutch. "But my mother was an Afrikaner," she said.

A surprised Moolman requested an explanation, and she responded, "Do you have time? It's a long story."

They left together, and as they sat at a street café the tale unfolded. Lucille had met the woman, whom she came to love as a mother, during the 1964 military hearings known as the Kwai River Tribunals. Lucille was one of the "comfort women", many of them children, who were held captive by the Japanese as sex slaves throughout the war. During the hearings, one of the specialist witnesses heard a vulnerable Javanese girl who was speaking Dutch, and took pity on her. Lucille was the Javanese girl; the specialist witness was Susan Nell.

That Friday night, Lucille from Ubon began to tell Nico Moolman the life story of Susan Nell. It was long and complex, and it would take another two evenings before it was completed. In Moolman's recounting of the tale, a bywoner's daughter named Susan Nell, whose entire family died in the Anglo-Boer War, was raped by two British officers and a joiner on 1 January 1902 in the Winburg concentration camp. Later, a Sotho man picked her up in the veld where she had fallen from the hearse wagon, and he and a woman nursed her back to health in a nearby cave until she was strong enough for the train journey to Cape Town. A fellow traveller, a photographer named Jack Perry, took pity on Susan and arranged for her to be taken care of by a well-known local philanthropist, Marie Koopmans-De Wet. She took the young woman under her wing, and Susan eventually ended up in the Netherlands, where she qualified as a psychiatric nurse.

While in Europe, Susan came across both her rapists, the first during The First World War in a military hospital in Devon, and the second during the Kwai River Tribunals held after the Second World War.

That is the story that a Javanese woman told Nico Mool-man over the course of three evenings in August 2009. Upon his return to South Africa, he adapted the story into a novel. He decided to write it in English so that those who were guilty of such crimes against him and his people could take note. Moolman self-published under the title *The Boer Whore*.

I came to hear of the book through one of my brothers, Charles Smith, who is a journalist. He felt it would be worth-while to investigate the possibility of an Afrikaans version. I put this to Riana Barnard of Tafelberg Publishers, and she was immediately receptive to the idea. She agreed with me though that a translation of *The Boer Whore* would not work, and that the factual framework should rather be used as the foundation for a new novel, which she asked me to write.

My book diverges from Moolman's in many respects. For one, I wanted to explore Susan Nell's inner life by means of a novelistic approach, and along the way explore how the con-frontation with one of her rapists may have played out.

While my narrative does not cover the entire span of Susan's life, it remains of interest to know what became of her. In South Africa, she seems to have left no trace of her life. It was not possible to get proof of her membership of the church in Ermelo, as the church and its archives burned down during the Anglo-Boer War. Moreover, the fact that her name does not appear in the official register of the Win-burg concentration camp is by no means exceptional. A large proportion of the deceased – estimated to be as high as twenty per cent – are simply described as "unknown".

What, then, was the fate of Susan Nell? In Moolman's account, she returned to the Netherlands after her last visit to South Africa in the 1950s. Barely three months later, she died of cancer. Her remains were repatriated, and Jack Perry saw to it that her ashes were scattered in accordance with instructions in her will. During her last visit to Winburg, Susan noticed that the grave next to that of her childhood friend, Alice Draper, was an empty unmarked grave. She believed that it was the grave assigned to her by the camp authorities – and that is where she wished her ashes to be scattered. And so that empty unmarked grave is hers.

Francois Smith
May 2014